Stranded
in Lake
Mistletoe

AMBER KELLY

Cover Design: Sommer Stein, Perfect Pear Creative Covers
Editor: Jovana Shirley, Unforeseen Editing, www.unforeseenediting.com
Proofreader: Autumn Gantz
Formatter: Champagne Book Design

To Emily, my favorite girl in the whole wide world. KK loves you to the moon and back a bazillion times.

Stranded
in Lake
Mistletoe

Prologue

Isaac
Six Years Ago

"I CAN'T BELIEVE YOU'RE LEAVING THREE DAYS BEFORE CHRISTMAS. What am I supposed to tell Cobie?"

The bitter chill of my wife, Lonnie's, words hang in the air as I pack my bags, preparing to leave behind the warmth of home and family for a new photojournalist assignment in Germany.

"It's one Christmas, and she's two years old. She won't even realize I'm gone," I say.

She crosses her arms over her chest and stands in the doorway. "That's not the point. I will. Your parents will."

I close the top of my suitcase and walk to her. "I'm sorry. I know this is horrible timing, but it's the first on-location assignment I've been offered, and I need to go. This is a good thing for us. For our future. This is big."

She sighs and plants her forehead against my chest. "I know you're right. It's just Christmas with our family is big too. I don't want you to miss the big stuff."

I kiss the top of her head. "One year. I promise. That's all. I just need my foot in the door."

She looks up at me. "Okay, one year."

The doorbell rings.

"Your chariot awaits."

She gives me a half-smile as she goes to answer the door.

I pick up suitcase and throw my camera bag over my shoulder.

Excitement washes over me as I head out to the taxi, but I can't shake the pang in my chest as I look back at Lonnie, holding a waving Cobie in her arms, knowing that this Christmas, my lens will capture stunning scenes far away from the cozy embrace of my family. For the first time, I'll miss the sparkle in Cobie's eyes as she unwraps her gifts, the sound of her giggles filling our living room.

But with every shutter click, I vow to freeze the moments I witness, not just for my camera and the magazine feature, but also for my heart, so when I return, I can share the world with her.

One frame at a time.

Chapter One

Isaac
Present

I HOLD COBIE'S HAND TIGHTLY AS I HELP HER DOWN FROM THE passenger side of the rented SUV.

The crisp air carries the scent of pine, and her eyes widen with excitement as she takes in the sight of our stopover on our way to Paris for Christmas.

"Daddy, it's so pretty here!" she exclaims, her small hand pointing toward the glistening lake across the road.

Her excitement is music to my ears. She's been rather melancholy since I picked her up yesterday, but the sight of snow perked her up on the ride from the airport.

Living in San Antonio, Texas, she has never seen snow falling in person before. When the flakes began to flutter around the SUV, I had to stop and pull over onto the side of the road so she could get out and touch it before we could continue.

I smile down at her, my heart filling with love for my moody little girl.

Lake Mistletoe is a holiday destination here in the Idaho Rockies. Nestled in the valley just down the mountainside of Sun Valley, it has grown in popularity over the past few years and has landed on the radar of *Epic Odysseys*, my employer and one of the largest international travel magazines in the world.

"It sure is, sweetheart. We're going to have a great time here," I say, ruffling her hair gently.

Cobie beams up at me, her freckled face lit up with joy.

As we walk toward the cozy inn the magazine booked for us, I can't help but feel a sense of peace settle over me. It's been a few years since I was able to spend the holidays with my daughter.

Her mother and I have a custody agreement in place that allows me to spend every other Christmas with Cobie, but work has caused me to be away most every December, and Lonnie and her new husband, Greg, have been playing Mrs. Claus and Santa in my stead.

Inside The Gingerbread Inn, we are met with the aroma of apple cider and freshly baked cookies.

A woman wearing a red sweater, Santa hat, and warm smile greets us, "Good afternoon. Welcome to The Gingerbread Inn."

"Hi, I'm Cobie, and this is my daddy," Cobie offers.

"It's nice to meet you, Cobie and Cobie's daddy. I'm Annette."

"Do you have cookies?" Cobie asks.

Annette grins and looks over the desk and down at my curious girl and whispers, "I'm pretty sure Miss Trixie just pulled a fresh batch from the oven. If you want to check out the room down the hall, the one with the big fireplace, I bet they're still warm."

Cobie leaves me standing at the front desk as she takes off to explore every nook and cranny of the inn with wide-eyed wonder.

I watch as she skips her way down a hallway and peeks around the corner. A squeal of glee fills the air. I chuckle.

She's growing up so fast, and moments like this are precious.

"I think she found the cookies," Annette says.

"I believe she has."

"Okay, Cobie's dad, how can I help you?"

"We have a reservation under Isaac Ralston," I reply.

She taps at her keyboard. "Yes, we have you in a double room for five nights. Is that correct?"

I nod.

She hands me a brass key on a fuzzy reindeer key chain. I twirl it around on my finger.

How long has it been since I was given an actual key for a room?

Most hotels or vacation rentals use key cards, mobile keys, or keyless touch-pad entry these days. The brass key adds to the charm of this live gingerbread house.

"You guys are in room 210. It's on the second floor. Just turn right at the top of the stairs. Dinner is served in the dining room at six, and you're in luck because our cook, Alice, is preparing her famous chicken 'n' dumplings tonight."

"That sounds amazing. I'm going to run out and grab our bags," I say.

Annette smiles. "No problem. I'll keep an eye on Cobie."

"Thank you."

I take another glance down the hallway before I head back out into the cold to fetch our luggage and my camera bag from the back of the SUV.

As I approach the vehicle, I hear a shout.

"Whoa!"

My head snaps to the snow-covered stairs at my left that lead above the garage, and I see a very pregnant woman struggling with a large plastic box.

Concerned, I quickly make my way over to help, carefully navigating the icy path to lend her a hand.

"Let me get that for you," I say as I take the load from her arms.

"Oh, thank you. I didn't realize it was so heavy. Keller would kill me if I slipped," she says.

I carry the box down to the landing, set it on the ground, and go back and extend my hand to help her down.

"I'm Willa, by the way. I own the inn," she introduces.

"Hi, Willa. I'm Isaac. I'm here to photograph the town for *Epic Odysseys*, and my daughter and I will be your guests for a few days."

She smiles. "Yes, the mayor told me to expect you. We're very excited to have our hometown featured in your magazine," she says as I lift the box again and follow her to the door.

I open it and wait for her to make it inside.

"Daddy, Daddy! They have hot cocoa and cookies in there," Cobie exclaims, as she comes running toward us.

"Slow down. Don't run," I call as she barrels into my legs.

"Do you want to have cocoa with me?" she asks as she looks up at me.

"I do. But I'm helping Miss Willa at the moment, and then I need to get our things from the car and take them to our room."

Her eyes slide to my right, where Willa is standing with her hand resting on her swollen belly.

"Is there a baby in your tummy?" Cobie asks.

"Yes, ma'am. A big baby boy, and I bet he'd love some cocoa and cookies," Willa answers.

Cobie steps back and looks at me. Then, she points down the hallway. "The cookies are that way. Meet us when you're done," she instructs.

"You got it, boss," I quip as I set the box on the reception desk.

She takes Willa's hand, and the two of them head to the treats.

I return outside to fetch our bags and carry them to our room.

It's a good size with two queen beds. There is a small sitting area to the left with a gliding rocker and a side table with a lamp in front of an Amish electric fireplace. There is a nightstand between the beds that holds a nostalgic ceramic Christmas tree with colorful bulbs. Two bottles of water and an ice bucket are sitting beside the television, which is perched upon a beautifully carved live-edge console. There's a sliding barn door that leads to a private bathroom.

I set my suitcase on the bed closest to the door and Cobie's pink suitcase on the other. I purchased it for her for her third birthday. It matches the one I bought for Lonnie with a plan to take them both on many great adventures.

Here we are, five years later, and it's the first time she's had the chance to use it.

"Wow, this is quite a spread," I say as we take a seat for dinner.

"Alice and Hal are the best. You won't find a finer meal in all of Lake Mistletoe." Harold Peterson, a frequent guest of the inn, whom I met earlier today, gives his opinion.

"Oh, Harold, thank you," Alice bellows.

Alice, the inn's cook, and her husband, Hal, wave off the compliment.

"It's the truth. My family and I have been coming here for over twenty years, and Alice's apple dumplings are one of the reasons why."

His grandsons, Brad and Jason, eagerly agree.

As we eat, all the patrons around the table reminisce about the years they've spent celebrating Christmas with Willa's grandparents, the former owners of the inn. Each one talking of the staff as if they were members of their family.

It's odd. How can people who are employed by a place you rent become so important to you? I've traveled to many destinations and stayed in some impressive places, but I don't think I could recall the name of a single front-desk clerk or cook at an establishment without looking back at my paperwork.

"So, Isaac, are you going to be here to enjoy the Christmas

Market?" Trixie—the inn's manager and mother of Willa's husband, Keller—asks.

"Oh, that would make for excellent photos for the article," Willa interjects.

"What's the Christmas Market?" Cobie asks.

"Every year, we have a tree-lighting festival with a holiday market. It's a lot of fun. There are games and sleigh rides around the lake, an ice-skating rink, and even a Christmas boat parade with prizes. Keller and Bob go all out with their decorations every year," Trixie explains.

"You should see what we have planned for this year," Bob—Trixie's husband and Keller's dad—adds.

Cobie's hopeful eyes come to me. "Can we go?"

"When is it?" I ask Trixie.

"Saturday after next. We'll be baking and crafting all week to prepare."

I look down at Cobie. "Sorry, kiddo, we're leaving for Paris on Sunday."

Her eyes fall to her plate, and she mumbles, "That's okay."

"Hey, Paris sounds like so much fun. I'm a little jealous," Willa chimes in.

"It does, and you guys will have a reason to come back next year," Trixie cajoles.

Cobie's disappointed eyes flitter to hers. "Yeah, I guess."

There's my melancholy girl again.

I look down at her. "We're going to have a great time while we are here, I promise."

"We can give you a list of highlights to check out," Willa offers.

"The mayor has set us up with a guide to show us around the town for a few days," I tell them.

"Perfect. And, Cobie, you might not be here for the market, but Alice and I would love some help getting ready for it. My grandchildren are coming over tonight to make wish bottles," Trixie says.

"You would?" Cobie beams.

"Absolutely."

"What are wish bottles?" she asks Trixie.

"Well, the story goes that, every year, good boys and girls in Lake Mistletoe can make a wish, and if they believe with all their hearts, then Santa will stir the water as his sleigh passes over on Christmas Eve, filling the lake with Christmas magic, and their wishes will be granted. This year, we are taking tiny glass bottles with cork stoppers and filling them with Christmas stars and snowflakes. Each kid will write their wish on a blank piece of paper and tuck it inside. We'll attach a red or green ribbon so you can hang your wish on the tree, where the magic is sure to find it," Trixie explains.

Cobie's eyes go wide. "Is that true?"

Lexie—one of the girls across the table, seated next to her mother—leans over and whispers to her, "My wish came true last year. If you want to make one before you leave, I'll keep it and hang it on the tree for you."

Cobie nods at her, and then her pleading eyes look up at me. "Can I help them, Daddy?"

I smile. "Sure, kiddo."

We finish dinner, which ends with coffee or milk and a mini gingerbread Bundt cake.

We say our good nights after dessert, and I take Cobie up to our room.

I put away our things as she takes a bath, brushes her teeth, and gets into her pajamas.

She climbs into her bed and burrows under the cozy covers.

I sit on the edge and tuck her in tight, ensuring she is snug and warm.

"Will you tell me a story, Daddy?" she asks.

"What kind of story do you want to hear?" I ask.

She answers through a yawn, "Tell me a story about Santa Claus."

I lie down beside her and prop myself against the headboard. I make up an adventurous tale of Santa and his reindeer crashing into and getting caught on the Eiffel Tower in Paris and Mrs. Claus coming to the rescue by sending a group of elves to help save Christmas.

Cobie's eyes get heavy with sleep, and before the elves make it to Santa's side, she is lightly snoring.

I kiss the top of her head, stand quietly, and head into the bathroom to shower the day away.

Chapter Two

Sela

I CAREFULLY BALANCE THE CARDBOARD TRAY IN ONE GLOVED HAND AS I use the other to open the heavy black iron door to town hall. I wave to the receptionist, Roxie, who is seated at the desk to the right.

She beams as I pluck a cup for her.

"What do we have this morning? Wait, let me guess," she says as she takes the cup and inhales. "Black tea with cinnamon and cloves?" she asks.

I shake my head. "Christmas tea with cacao nibs, clementine, and Mrs. Beatty's secret Christmas spice blend."

"Oh boy, thank you."

I pull two packets of brown sugar from my pocket for her and proceed to hurry down the hallway.

"Your peppermint mocha," I say as I hand off one of the coffees to Gillian as I pass the post office counter.

"You're a godsend, Sela," Gillian calls after me.

I continue on my way, stopping by Sheriff Watson's office to deliver his secretary, Patricia's, bagel and cream cheese.

I come to a halt in front of the door at the end of the hallway. I knock lightly before entering the mayor's office, the remaining steaming takeaway mugs of holiday lattes in my hand. The aroma of freshly brewed beans fills the room as I set the tray down on the edge of the large mahogany desk.

The mayor, Hoyt Miller, is on the phone, and I begin to tiptoe backward until he raises a finger to ask me to wait for a moment.

I started working for the mayor's office this summer after graduating from the University of Idaho Boise, where I'd studied interior architecture design. My dream is to be a museum technician and conservator right here in Lake Mistletoe. There is so much rich history in our small town and many talented local artisans.

Mayor Miller and I have worked hard to find the right location to build a museum to collect, preserve, interpret, and display that history and local art for generations to come, and now, we are fighting to secure funding for it.

He clicks off his call, and I hand him one of the lattes.

He takes a sip, closes his eyes, and sighs. "Tart, but so good."

"I'm glad you like it. Mrs. Beatty at the coffee shop is trying some new flavors this week. Today's special is white chocolate and cranberry latte."

He takes another sip and sets the cup to the side as he motions for me to take a seat.

I grab the other coffee and settle into the soft tobacco-colored leather chair in front of his desk.

"Sela, I need you to do me a favor. A travel magazine is sending a journalist to town to write an article about Lake Mistletoe," he begins.

"That's wonderful!"

"Yes, it is. I'm planning to devote most of my time next week to her and give her a history lesson about the town, but the photographer who will be capturing the photos that will accompany the article online and in the print copies had to come early because of a planned European trip for the holidays. He arrived yesterday, and he's coming in this morning. Unfortunately, I'll be busy overseeing the setup and decorating for the tree lighting the next few days, so I need you to show him around town."

"Okay. Anywhere in particular you want him to see?" I ask.

He raises a hand and swirls it in the air. "Oh, you know, downtown, the inns on the other side of the lake, the park, the skating rink, places like that. Just give him the grand tour, show him everything that you find captivating in town this time of year and introduce him around."

"You got it, boss," I agree.

"Thanks, Sela. It'll be a big help. His name is Isaac Ralston. He'll be here at ten. I'm headed out now to meet Bob at the hardware store to load up supplies. Please give Isaac my apologies and let him know that I'm eagerly anticipating meeting him tomorrow."

He stands, and I follow suit and walk with him to the door. I tell Roxie to ring my office when Isaac Ralston shows, and then I run to make a few calls and get a game plan together ahead of his arrival.

My phone chimes promptly at ten o'clock with Roxie letting me know Isaac has arrived.

I finish the spreadsheet I'm working on for the Lake Conservation Society meeting on Thursday and close down my computer. I grab my purse from my desk drawer, pull on my red wool wrap coat over my navy pantsuit, and wind the holly-print scarf my mother knit for me last year around my neck.

Clicking off the light and locking up my office, I make my way out to reception to greet him.

I spot him across the lobby. A tall figure with dark hair, he is wearing a cream cable-knit sweater, dark jeans, and brown boots. A black leather bag with a thick strap is slung over his shoulder, and his eyes are hidden behind a pair of aviator sunglasses.

His attention is cast down toward the little girl in a white coat, purple mittens, and snow boots. She has the same dark hair, hers in bouncing curls, and has her arm wrapped around his left leg.

I take a deep breath and make my way to them.

"Hi. Are you Isaac?" I ask.

He lifts his glasses and pulls them to rest atop his damp hair, revealing stormy-gray eyes that crinkle at the corners as he smiles warmly.

Oh my.

"Yes, I am. You must be Sela Prince."

His voice is husky and captivating and sends a shiver down my spine.

He extends his arm, and I move closer. His large hand envelops mine.

"Yes, it's nice to meet you. And who do we have here? Let me guess … she's your assistant?" I ask as my eyes fall to his tiny companion.

The girl giggles. "No, silly. I'm too little," she says.

"This is my daughter, Cobie. I hope it's okay if she joins us today."

I release his hand and bend down to her eye level.

"Of course it's okay. It's lovely to meet you, Cobie. We're going to have a lot of fun together."

She grins and looks up at her dad.

He winks at her, and she turns back to me.

"I like your scarf," she says.

"Thank you. I like your mittens," I return and then stand and look between them. "Shall we get this tour started?"

"Are we going to see Santa Claus?" Cobie asks.

"Santa?" I ask in surprise.

Isaac sighs. "The innkeeper where we're staying told her to keep her eyes open because Santa has a vacation cottage hidden somewhere in Lake Mistletoe and you never know when you'll run into him."

"Innkeeper?" I ask.

"Yes, we're staying at The Gingerbread Inn across the lake," he replies.

"Ah, I see. Miss Trixie has been spilling all our town secrets again," I say as I watch Cobie's eyes light up. "Santa is an elusive character, and he doesn't make it easy to find him, but this weekend is the candlelit town stroll, where we go from shop to shop, looking for his elves."

"Elves?"

"Yes, ma'am. They come to hide treats and mistletoe all over town for boys and girls to find. Now, no one is sure that Santa will be accompanying the elves, but hopefully, we'll get lucky and catch a glimpse of the big guy," I explain.

Cobie lets go of her father's leg and joins me in front of him. "Can we search for elves, Daddy?"

His hand goes to the back of his neck, and he purses his mouth. Then, his eyes move from his daughter to me.

"What day is the stroll?" he asks.

"Friday evening at sunset."

He blows out a breath and nods. "We'll be here until Sunday, and I'd like to see if I can catch a few of those elves on camera."

Cobie jumps up and down. "Yay!"

He smiles at her, and I can see his joy at her delight.

"Well, shall we get today's tour started? First stop is the coffee shop to meet Mrs. Beatty and check out her hot cocoa bar," I prompt.

Cobie reaches her mitten-covered hand up to take mine.

I tell Roxie to forward any pressing calls to my cell as Isaac opens the door and holds it wide.

I lead the three of us out onto the sidewalk and into the falling snow toward our first festive destination.

Chapter Three

Isaac

I FALL INTO STEP BEHIND THE GIRLS AS COBIE CHATTERS AWAY WITH our tour guide, telling her all about her baby brother who was born over the summer.

"Is he back at the inn?" Sela asks.

"No, silly. He's at home with Mommy and his daddy," Cobie explains.

Sela looks over her shoulder at me in confusion.

"Cobie's stepfather, Greg," I clarify.

"Oh, I see." She looks back down at Cobie. "Brothers are the best. I have a big brother, and he is my best friend."

"All my brother does is sleep, poop, and cry," Cobie states.

Sela laughs. It's a melodic sound that floats in the air and wraps around me.

"He'll outgrow that soon, and I'm sure you two will be the best of friends one day too."

We continue walking down the sidewalk, passing storefronts decorated for the holidays.

I take my camera from the bag on my hip and begin to snap candid shots of the serene and magical scene.

The town is hushed, enveloped in a soft white blanket of fresh powder, but there is an underlying buzz of anticipation as window shades are raised for the day and lights hanging in all the storefront windows blink to life, casting a gentle glow and creating a surreal holiday vibe. The girls' steps are met with a satisfying crunch beneath their feet.

The cold, crisp air makes my cheeks tingle as I focus the lens on the buildings that wear a coat of glistening snow, creating a sense of peaceful isolation.

People hurry by, bundled up in snug winter coats, their breath visible in the chilly air. The falling snowflakes dance and twirl around them, catching the light and creating a shimmering effect that adds a touch of magic to the cozy landscape.

Sela brings us to a halt in front of a large red door. "Welcome to The Snug Mug. The best coffeehouse around," she insists.

We follow her into the shop to a delightful sight. The space is filled with a warm and festive holiday spirit.

The moment you step inside, you're greeted by the comforting aroma of freshly brewed coffee, mingling with hints of cinnamon and spice.

There's a tall Christmas tree in one corner, adorned with an array of ornaments—shiny balls painted with coffee mugs and pots, delicate glitter-covered marshmallows, and strings of coffee beans and cranberries. Beneath the tree is an assortment of coffee-themed gifts with bright bows—from a travel mug to an espresso machine.

Wreaths made of fragrant pine branches, red ribbons, and pine cones line the wall that leads to the counter, where a round, silver-haired barista is working her magic.

The bar is framed with a garland of pine and holly, and the cash register is surrounded by a collection of nutcrackers.

The menu board showcases a handwritten script of seasonal delights, like peppermint mocha and gingerbread latte.

Welcoming, plush armchairs and sofas are arranged around low coffee tables, inviting customers to sit and savor their drinks as soft, instrumental Christmas music plays in the background. Customers, wrapped in scarves and gloves, chat and laugh as they enjoy the homey ambiance.

Sela and Cobie greet the barista while I take snaps of a couple cuddling on the sofa by the fireplace. The woman has her eyes closed and a soft smile on her lips as her companion wraps an arm around her shoulders and kisses her temple. Then another of a young woman blowing the rim of a snowman-themed mug before dropping two marshmallows inside and handing it over to a wide-eyed boy.

"Isaac?"

I turn at the sound of my name.

"Would you like anything?" Sela asks.

I scan the menu above her. "Yes, I'll take a spiced chai latte, please."

"Would you like it dirty?" the barista asks.

"Dirty?"

"With a shot of espresso?"

"I think I would like it extra dirty."

A tinge of pink brightens the woman's cheeks.

"Oh, I like this one," she tells Sela before turning to the machines at her back to create our orders.

Cobie bounces over to me with a snowman mug of her own in hand. "Daddy, can you help me?"

We make our way over to the carefully curated hot cocoa bar, nestled in the corner left of the fireplace.

The bar is impressive with a large, steaming pot of velvety hot chocolate, emitting a tantalizing aroma. Surrounding the pot is an array of toppings. Whipped cream in a dispenser. Marshmallows in different shapes, sizes, and colors, ranging from classic to gourmet flavors, like caramel or peppermint. There are bowls filled with crushed candy canes, chocolate shavings, and cinnamon sticks for that extra touch.

To accompany the hot cocoa, there are plates of freshly baked cookies, brownies, and pastries, as well as bowls of strawberries and melon.

A selection of flavored syrups—like caramel, hazelnut, or peppermint—is available, allowing guests to customize their beverages.

I take the mug from Cobie, carefully fill it with hot chocolate, and set it on the bar. Then, I step back and photograph her as she adds a dollop of cream and sprinkles crushed peppermint on top.

Sela joins us with a cup and saucer in each hand.

I relieve her of one, and we take a seat at the booth tucked beside the front window.

Cobie tugs off her mittens and sets them on the table so she can better grip the handle of the mug.

"We're going to have to detox you from cocoa when we leave," I tell her as her tongue darts out and licks the red-and-white-speckled whipped topping.

I look across to Sela. "Trixie had a cup waiting for her when we came down for breakfast this morning."

She shrugs. "There's no such thing as too much cocoa or too many Christmas lattes this time of year. You're allowed to indulge without guilt during the holidays."

Cobie agrees, and I chuckle at her observation.

"So, where are we headed to next?" I ask.

Sela thinks for a moment and grins.

"A hidden gem."

We finish our refreshments and make our way back outside. Sela leads us across the street and down a couple of blocks to an unassuming building nestled amid bustling Main Street businesses.

Keller Harris Design Studio is stenciled on the door.

"Keller Harris—isn't that Willa's husband?" I ask.

"He is."

"We met at the inn last night," I say.

"This is the shop he and my brother own. Keller is a master craftsman who makes hand-carved furniture, and my brother is an artist who does the custom carvings or paintings that their customers request. He also creates wood and metal sculptures and hand-made snow globes. They happen to be working on something extra special at the moment. I thought we could take a peek," she says as she opens the door.

A bell chimes as we walk into a large showroom.

"Wow, these are amazing," I muse as I take in the variety of sample furniture on display.

"Right? They can take any of these and create unique designs to a customer's specifications. People who visit Lake Mistletoe fall in love and place orders that ship all over the country." Sela beams.

"She's biased," a deep voice booms, and we turn to see a dark-haired man with the same steel-blue eyes as Sela coming through a pair of swinging doors.

"Doesn't make it any less true," she quips.

The man comes to a stop in front of her, and she steps in and wraps him in a warm embrace.

"Hi, sis," he says as he taps a kiss to her forehead.

She releases him and introduces us. "This is Isaac Ralston and his daughter, Cobie. Isaac, this is my brother, Brannigan Prince."

He extends his hand. "You can call me Bran."

I shake his offered hand as Sela continues, "Isaac is a photographer who is in town to take pictures for a story the travel magazine he works for is doing on Lake Mistletoe."

"Yeah, Keller mentioned that," Bran says.

"Hoyt asked me to show them around today, and I thought we could start here. Anyway, can we get a sneak peek at the project you guys are working on?" she asks, her eyes pleading.

"I don't know. It's a top-secret project that Santa himself ordered. Can you guys be trusted?" he asks, bringing his gaze to Cobie and raising a questioning brow.

Cobie's eyes go wide, and she looks up at Sela.

"Absolutely. I can vouch for her," Sela says.

"Okay, follow me."

He leads us into the back to what looks like a workshop.

"We don't let just anyone see behind the curtain. Only the very special people," he teases.

In the center of the room stands a large structure, covered with a massive brown tarp.

Bran takes one of the corners and pulls the covering free to expose what lies beneath.

A hand-carved, life-sized Santa sleigh.

Cobie squeals at the sight.

The sleigh is expertly carved from sturdy wood with every curve and contour meticulously shaped to perfection. The wood glows with a rich, warm finish, highlighting the natural grains and textures. Intricate detailing adorns the entire surface of the sleigh, including playful elves, prancing reindeer, and snow-covered pine trees. Each carving is done with precision and care, bringing the entire sleigh to life.

I raise my camera. "May I?" I ask Bran.

"Sure, just don't show anyone until after the tree lighting," he requests.

"It'll stay under wraps until the article comes out in a few weeks," I promise.

I check the camera's settings and focus and make a circle around the piece of art.

At the front of the sleigh, there's a spacious seat, where Santa would sit, carved and covered in white upholstery cushions with gold threading. The backrest has a plush red velvet cushion, ensuring that Santa can relax as he embarks on his magical journey. The armrests are embellished with patterns of holly and jingle bells, adding to the festive charm.

The sleigh rests on sturdy bronze blades, no doubt to ensure smooth travels for Santa and his reindeer.

"The attention to detail in the carving is remarkable," I observe as I click frame after frame.

Running along the edges of the sleigh are real jingle bells, and tiny, twinkling LED lights are intricately woven into the woodwork.

"Do the lights work?" I ask.

"Let's see," Bran says as he walks over to a switch and flips it. Then, he presses a button beside the sleigh steering wheel. The lights blink on, and a soft glow illuminates the wooden sleigh, as if it were alight with Christmas magic.

"Wow," Cobie mutters.

"Do you think the big guy is going to like it?" Bran asks Cobie, and she gives him an enthusiastic nod. "Me too. There is one thing I could use your help with though."

Cobie's eyes go to him.

"I'm not sure how comfortable it is. We can't have Santa with a stiff back and sore bum. Would you mind trying it out for me?" he asks.

Cobie's arms shoot straight up. Bran chuckles as he lifts her off her feet and sets her on the sleigh seat.

I capture every moment of her wonder and delight as she runs her hands over the armrests and clutches the wheel.

"What do you think? Will Santa be comfy all night on Christmas Eve?" Bran asks.

"Yeah, but he needs a cupholder for hot chocolate to keep him warm in the sky," she suggests.

"A cupholder," Bran repeats as he rubs his chin. "I think you're right. Thank you for the suggestion."

Cobie beams at him.

The bell on the door chimes again, and Bran's eyes go wide. He plucks Cobie from the seat and sets her back on her feet before clicking off the lights and tossing the tarp back on top.

Keller walks into the workshop just as Bran switches the overhead lights back on.

Bran looks at Cobie and places a finger over his lips.

Keller's hands go to his hips.

"What's going on in here?" he asks.

"Nothing," the four of us say in unison.

Chapter Four

Sela

KELLER SHOWS US A FEW FURNITURE DESIGNS HE IS WORKING ON while Bran introduces Cobie to the art of glass blowing.

"This is what I'm working on for Willa for Christmas," he says.

"Oh, Keller, it's incredible. Willa is going to love it," I say.

I walk around the custom-built crib with carved baby animals and the family name in each end panel.

"What wood did you use on this?" Isaac asks.

"Knotty alder. It's a bit softer than other hard woods, which makes it easier to shape and stain, but it's still strong," Keller replies.

"It's beautiful. I love the baby animals," I praise.

"Bran did those. He's painting a mural on the nursery wall to match. Willa wants it to look like a magical safari."

Isaac snaps a few shots of the custom work.

"What's that over there?" he asks.

Keller's eyes follow his to a structure against the far wall. "That is the new barn set display we made for the live nativity at the church. Last year, a few shepherds fell through the floor, so we built a new platform and decided to go ahead and give the barn and manger a facelift."

"Live nativity? When is that?" Isaac asks.

"Saturday afternoon. Would you like to come? Bran is playing Joseph again this year, and his girlfriend, Hannah, will be making her debut as Mary," I say.

"I'd love to. Dawn and Daniel will be here on Saturday, and I'm sure she'll want to cover it for the article," he says.

"Dawn and Daniel?" Keller asks.

"Dawn is the journalist who will be writing the article for the magazine. She and her husband are supposed to arrive late afternoon."

"I thought you were doing the article," Keller says, confused.

"No, I'm not a journalist. I couldn't write my way out of a box. I just take the pictures."

Cobie comes running up with Bran on her heels.

"Look, Daddy, I made a friendship ball!" She holds up the multi-colored blown glass ornament for Isaac to see.

"Wow, great job, kiddo," he praises.

"Bran said we have to hang it in a window so the light can catch the colors, and it will attract friendship and good luck," she explains.

"We can never have too much of either," he says.

She hands it over to him. "Here, this one is for your house. We're gonna make another one for Mommy's house," she says.

"I'm not sure we have much room in our suitcases, and these are awfully fragile to carry all the way to Paris with us," he says.

Her face falls. "Oh, right."

I step between them. "I'd be happy to send them to you. Once you're home from your trip. You can leave them with me, and I'll look after them while you're gone and then package them carefully and ship them to you," I offer.

Cobie smiles and thanks me, then skips off to make another ornament.

"I appreciate you offering to do that," Isaac whispers as we watch her go.

"It's no problem at all. The post office is literally outside my office door."

"It's still generous."

Keller accompanies us to our next stop. His sister Norah's flower shop.

We walk in, and Norah greets us from behind the counter.

"Hi, Sela, Keller. Who are your friends?" she asks.

"I'm Cobie Ralston, and that's my daddy. He wants to take your picture," Cobie replies.

"He does?"

"Yeah, he takes pictures of everything."

Norah's amused eyes flitter to us. "Hmm, well, how do I look?"

She twirls so we can see her red leggings and oversize sweater with the words *I Love a Man with a Beard* wrapped around a headshot of Santa.

"I like your sweater," Cobie says.

"We're going to be best friends, aren't we?" Norah asks her.

Cobie giggles.

Isaac snaps a photo as she leans over the counter to hand Cobie a candy cane. Then, he begins to look around the quaint shop.

Wreaths made of vibrant red bows and lush greenery hang on the walls, and potted evergreens line the shelves.

The scent of fresh pine mingles with the fragrant aroma of roses. A Christmas tree—covered in holly branches, mistletoe, poinsettia blooms, frosted pine cones, and delicate flower-print ribbons—stands proudly in front of the window that overlooks the sidewalk. Its base is surrounded by bouquets of white lilies and crimson carnations.

Isaac marvels at the artful combination of blooms and Christmas decor, making the shop burst with Christmas joy.

"Thank you. That's quite the compliment, coming from a world-famous photographer," Norah says.

"I don't know about that famous part, but I know beauty when I see it," he states.

Norah, who is now standing beside me, leans over and whispers in my ear, "I know beauty when I see it, too, and that man is beautiful."

I shove my elbow into her side, and she yelps.

"You're Mr. Keller's sister?" Cobie asks Norah.

"I am indeed."

"We're staying at his house. Miss Trixie and I are making wishing bottles tonight after dinner."

"You are? Miss Trixie is my momma, and I help her make crafts all the time," Norah says.

"You can come help us tonight," Cobie suggests.

"I might just do that. I'll have to call and see what Alice has planned for dinner," Norah replies.

"It's pot roast night," Keller interjects.

Norah scowls. "Again? We just had pot roast a couple of days ago."

Keller shrugs. "Willa says the baby loves Alice's pot roast, so Alice insists on making all the pot roast she can eat until he comes."

"Fine, if we must." Norah looks down at Cobie. "Alice's roast is the best."

"So, you'll come?"

"I will. Maybe we can talk Sela here into coming, too, and we'll make it a party."

"Yeah, that sounds like the best idea ever," Cobie squeals.

Keller looks at Isaac. "A crafts party? Yikes. Do you want to join me and Pop after dinner? We're going to be drinking beer and working on our parade boat in my parents' garage."

Isaac glances at his daughter. "I don't know. I don't want to leave Cobie for the girls to look after," he says.

"Oh, please, you'll just be in our way," Norah says.

"Yeah, Daddy," Cobie agrees, throwing her hands in the air in mock frustration.

"Okay, fine. I'm all yours, Keller."

Keller slaps him on the back. "Thanks. Pop has come up with a complicated design this year, and we can use all the help we can get."

Keller pays Norah for the poinsettias Willa ordered for the inn, and Isaac helps him carry them across the street to his truck while Cobie and I run a package that was delivered this afternoon up to my apartment, which is above the flower shop.

Norah rented it to me when I returned from school. She and her husband, Sammy, built a house next to her and Keller's sister Donna last year.

Once Isaac returns, the three of us say our good-byes to Norah and continue our walk through town.

"See you guys tonight," Norah calls as she waves us off.

Cobie walks ahead of us as she enjoys the candy cane.

"So, what do you think so far?" I ask.

"I can see the appeal of Lake Mistletoe. I love the mixture of old and new architecture and how everyone decorates to their niche."

"You noticed that, did you?"

"Yeah. My favorite is the tree in Keller and Bran's shop with the power tool ornaments and chain links hanging from the branches."

"Fun, right? I don't mean to brag, but Norah and I made the tape measure garland for them," I tell him.

"Nice touch," he praises.

"Bran might be the artist in the family, but I can occasionally make cool things too. In fact, the space up ahead to the right is where I plan to create the coolest thing in town," I inform him.

As we approach, he reads the signage attached to the front of the stone building.

Future site of The Lake Mistletoe Heritage and History Museum.

He raises a brow. "A museum?"

"Yep. It's my passion project. I've dreamed of opening a museum in Lake Mistletoe for years, showcasing the rich history and artistry of our town. A place where people can come together to learn, appreciate, and celebrate our heritage with interactive exhibits and galleries dedicated to local artists. I can see children laughing and learning, families bonding over shared history. A place that brings our community together."

"Looks like it's about to come to fruition," he says.

"Maybe. There are a lot of things that have to fall into place for it to happen. We have the location. We've applied for a state funding grant, and I've also solicited private funding. In fact, this year's Holly Ball is sponsoring our efforts."

"What's the Holly Ball?" he asks.

"It's an annual ball that the town throws the day before Christmas Eve. All the grown-ups get to dress up and dance the night away. There's food and cocktails and door prizes. All the ticket sales go to the Lake Mistletoe conservation fund, which helps maintain the lake, pedestrian bridge, and the walking trail. But this year, a portion of the ticket sales and the proceeds from a silent auction are being set aside for the museum project."

He nods. "This town really comes together, doesn't it?"

"We do. When something is important to one of us, it somehow becomes important to us all," I agree.

"I like that. You don't get that type of camaraderie in big cities. Some philanthropists lend their names to certain charities and the like, and there is a fundraiser every other day, but it becomes more of a social status thing than anything else."

"Hmm, I guess as long as the ones in need get the funds, that's all that matters in the end, isn't it?" I ask.

"I suppose," he mutters.

Cobie stops at the bakery, where an impressive gingerbread re-creation of the North Pole is displayed in the front window.

"Daddy, look," she calls as she points to the sweet structure. "It's where Santa Claus lives," she cries.

Isaac instinctively reaches for his camera, and we go inside to visit with Mr. Bridgeman and admire his talent.

We find him punching holes in a cooling rack of gingerbread men and threading them with hooks for the Christmas tree by the display case.

Cobie sits on one of the barstools and chats away with him while Isaac walks around and snaps images of the bakery, the window display, and a few of the customers as they look over the confections in the case and make their selections.

We leave with a box of cookies and slices of yule log.

"You've had a successful day, kiddo—hot cocoa, friendship balls, candy canes, and a box of baked goods." He ticks off her wares.

"Everyone is so nice here, and they have the best bakery," she muses.

"You know, they have amazing bakeries in Paris too. Wait until you taste the macarons. They're perfection," he tells her.

"Yeah, you said," she mumbles.

We make it to the end of the sidewalk just as my phone chimes with a message.

I fish it out of my purse and notice the time says 4:43.

"Where did the time go? It's almost five," I inform them.

"And we only made it down one street," Isaac muses.

"I know. I have so much more to show you guys, but I need to get back to my office and do a few things before I head to the inn for pot roast."

"Would you be available for round two tomorrow?" he asks.

"I'll have to check with the mayor, but I'm sure I can clear some time on my schedule so we can start bright and early."

The two of them walk me back to town hall before we say our good-byes.

I watch at the door until they are out of sight.
Roxie strides up behind me.
"That is one tall, sexy drink of water," she says.
"Roxie," I scold.
"What? I'm married, not dead," she says.

Chapter Five

Isaac

THE INN IS BUSTLING WITH ACTIVITY WHEN WE RETURN. GUESTS are checking in at the front desk, children are laughing and singing in the great room as Trixie plays the piano, Alice and Hal are setting the dining room up for dinner, and Keller is carrying firewood in through the back door.

Cobie asks to join the other children.

"You have schoolwork to do," I remind her.

She frowns.

Cobie is homeschooled by her mother. It's been a point of contention between the two of us. I feel that she needs to be in a public-school setting to acquire the benefits of socialization while Lonnie feels she'll be free to express herself and her feelings more openly at home. We compromised by agreeing that she would be homeschooled until she reached double digits, and then we would let her decide for herself.

The upside is that homeschooling allows her to travel with me for these four weeks, but I did promise that she would keep up with her studies.

"If you knock the work out now, your entire evening will be free to spend with Trixie and the other ladies," I remind her.

"Yes, I'd better get my math done before dinner," she decides.

I follow her up to our room and set her up on the laptop so she can video-chat with her mother and baby brother and go over today's assignment. Then, I head back downstairs to offer Keller help with the firewood.

"Thanks. Pop dropped a cord off in the back. I'm stacking them in the great room and out by the firepit so the girls have plenty."

He leads me out a door and into the back of the inn.

"Whoa, this space is something else," I say as I take in the yard encased by glass panels.

"It's Willa's garden atrium. The glass retracts during the spring and summer to open it up to the warm weather and rain. This time of year, it's closed so guests can sit out here and watch the snow fall around them. Mom and Willa string it with lights and fill it with all the festive decor," he explains.

I wish I had my camera.

There are so many interesting things to capture in Lake Mistletoe.

"I can see why this town is such a draw for holiday travelers," I muse.

He nods. "It is magical this time of year."

"What about the rest of the year?" I ask.

"We thrive, like anywhere else. We still get a steady stream of visitors. Families come to enjoy the lake in the spring and summer. They swim, kayak, paddleboard, and fish. Bran started a new rock-climbing club, and he and Mayor Miller have plans for a zip line that will run from the crest of the mountain all the way down to the lake. The town offers some great hiking trails, and in the fall, when the leaves turn beautiful colors, we have hayrides, corn mazes, and pumpkin patches," he says. "But in the winter, once the snow begins to fall, Sun Valley opens to skiers, which is extra special."

I try to imagine the town in bloom and with sunbathers on the bank of the lake.

"I think, in my mind, Lake Mistletoe is a place that only exists during the holidays. Like the North Pole," I say.

Keller chuckles. "Nope. We're here year-round, working, playing, loving, and living. You should see the haunted gingerbread house Willa and Mom turn this place into for Halloween."

I make a mental note to have Dawn add that information to the article.

We carry wood out to the firepit, and then I help him stack the rest in the shed out by the garage.

Norah and Sela arrive together a few moments later.

"Hey, Keller, can you carry the boxes from the backseat inside?" Norah asks.

We walk over to the Jeep as she opens the door.

"What is all this stuff?" Keller asks.

"It's samples that Hannah sent for Trixie and Willa's approval," Sela answers as she joins us.

Her hair is in a low ponytail, and her face is freshly washed. She's wearing a white long-sleeved shirt with a low neckline and a pair of faded jeans that hugs her curves. Her feet are snug inside of dark brown leather hiking boots.

It's a striking difference from the pulled-together professional look of this morning.

Sexy.

I like it.

"Samples of what?" Keller asks, dragging me from my wayward thoughts.

Norah shrugs. "Baby shower stuff. They finally decided on a theme, and now, they are narrowing down fabric for the table coverings and flowers for the centerpiece arrangements," Norah informs.

"Fabric? Are they hand-making the tablecloths? We have a ton in storage already that we use for events."

"No tablecloths. We're making sheer, gauzy runners for the middle of the tables. With the jungle theme, Hannah thinks the sage green and apricot orange would work best, but Willa mentioned light blue and yellow, so Hannah sent swatches of each for her to look at," Norah explains.

"I have no idea what a gauzy runner is. Do you?" Keller asks, turning to me.

"Not a clue," I concur.

Keller and I both grab hold of a box and follow the girls inside the inn. Sela explains that Hannah is her brother's girlfriend who moved to Lake Mistletoe from Las Vegas and opened her own event planning company last year.

"She just upped and moved from Vegas? That must have been a culture shock. I can't imagine she is as busy."

Sela grins. "I think Bran might have been a factor in the decision, but we have our share of events here in Lake Mistletoe. She stays busy, trust me."

"And what about you? Are you happy to be back, or do you miss Boise?" I ask.

"I won't lie. I enjoyed my time in the city, but there's no place like home. I'm sure you know what I mean, seeing as you travel so much. Don't you love it when you get to go home?"

I shrug.

The truth is, the only thing that excites me about going back to San Antonio after a trip is Cobie.

We settle in to enjoy a meal of roast with red potatoes and baby carrots.

"This is the best roast I've ever had. What is in this gravy?" I ask Alice.

"It's a secret. She won't tell any of us," Willa gripes.

"I know there's red wine in it. I've walked in and seen her add it to the pan drippings," Norah says.

"But the rub she does before browning the meat is the key, and she won't tell me what it is," Willa states.

"She mixes the rub herself. I don't even know what's in it," Hal informs.

I help Cobie squirt a pile of ketchup on her meat, smash a couple of potatoes, and pour gravy over the top.

Everyone chats animatedly as we eat.

It's a funny thing; we've only been here for a couple of days, and yet it feels like we're breaking bread with old friends.

Cobie and Lexie are excited about the planned evening activities while the boys are discussing their plans to camp in the atrium tonight.

"You guys had better pull out all the stops this year because I have it on good authority that Bran and our dad are working on an entry for the boat parade," Sela tells Keller.

"I had my suspicion when he made up an excuse not to help us tonight," Keller muses.

"They've even recruited Sammy to help," Norah informs.

"Sammy? He's one of us," Bob points out.

"Yep. He says that Bran is an artist, so he figures they have an advantage," Norah explains.

"Traitor," Bob mumbles.

Willa shakes her head. "No name-calling. It's supposed to be a friendly competition," she reminds them.

"More like cutthroat," Norah mutters.

Once our plates are clean, Alice and Trixie bring out today's themed dessert of gingerbread pear loaf.

It's divine.

Keller, Bob, and I help Hal clear the table while the ladies get set up in the great room.

After building them a fire, we say our good-byes and pile into Keller's truck to head to work, my camera bag in my lap.

A gentleman, looking to be about Bob's age, meets us at Bob and Trixie's garage.

"Isaac, this is my old friend, Hoyt Miller. He brought supplies from the hardware store he owns in town," Bob introduces.

"As in Mayor Hoyt Miller?" I ask.

"One and the same," Hoyt replies.

"It's nice to meet you, Mr. Mayor," I tell him.

"You too. I'm sorry I was unable to get away today. I hope you enjoyed your afternoon in town," he says as we follow Bob and Keller inside.

"We did, although we have much more to see. Sela was a great tour guide."

He nods. "Yes, I knew I was putting you in capable hands, and I have no doubt you'll get everything you need," he agrees.

Bob leads us over to a small red boat on a pedestal in the right bay of the garage.

"What's this year's theme?" Keller asks his father.

Walking over to a drafting table, Bob unrolls a set of blueprints and spreads them out before us. "I want to build a floating platform under the boat so it appears to be hovering over the water. Then, I want to attach a set of wires wrapped in lights to eight giant sturgeons that are suspended in the air with one in the front that has a glowing red point in the nose. We'll set an inflatable Santa inside."

I look down at the carefully crafted plan in wonder.

"Santa's boat pulled by fish instead of Santa's sleigh pulled by reindeer. That's brilliant," I praise.

Bob grins. "If we can pull it off," he agrees.

"You guys enter the parade contest every year?" I ask.

"Since I was a boy. My grandfather and father started the tradition.

Then, when I had children of my own, I continued it. This will be my fifty-fifth entry," Bob reveals.

"And his twenty-fifth blue ribbon," Keller adds.

"Fingers crossed," Bob concurs.

The three of them roll their sleeves up and get to work while I grab my camera and capture every element—from Keller cutting the wooden frame for the Styrofoam platform, Hoyt measuring and cutting the thick black wire from a large spool, and Bob boring a hole into the tip of one of the plastic sturgeon's noses to feed the red light bulb through.

They move together with familiar ease as they make the blueprint come to life before my eyes.

Once the boat is secured to the frame, Bob takes a step back to admire the progress.

"What do you think, Pop?" Keller asks as he slings an arm over his father's shoulders.

"I believe we have another blue ribbon in our future."

Chapter Six

Sela

I DUCK MY CHIN INTO THE COLLAR OF MY COAT AS I RUSH OUT OF THE flower shop. The soles of my snow boots grip the slippery concrete as I hurry down the sidewalk to town hall.

I'm running late.

It's not something I do.

Last night, we had a great time making wishing bottles for the market. The kids worked hard, and Trixie and Alice ended up with ten dozen bottles to sell.

Once we finished and tidied up our mess, Norah and I stayed with Cobie and let Trixie, Alice, and Willa retire while we waited for Keller to return with Isaac.

By the time they walked into the great room, where the three of us were watching *The Grinch*, Cobie was fast asleep.

Isaac picked her up and carried her to bed. Keller, worried about us driving so late in the snow, convinced Norah and me to catch a few hours of sleep on the couch. He threw two large logs on the fire and brought us pillows and extra blankets before going home in search of Willa.

We woke to the sound of Hal working in the kitchen, preparing breakfast.

He sent us off with freshly baked bacon and egg biscuits and to-go coffees.

Norah dropped me off at my apartment before hurrying home to get ready for her day. Luckily, she had her employee, Steph, scheduled to open the store.

I make it to the office, and Roxie stands to greet me, hands me a warm mug, and informs me that Isaac has already arrived and he and Hoyt are waiting for me in the mayor's office.

"Thanks, Roxie," I call as I hasten down the walkway leading to the mayor's office.

I knock once before entering to find Hoyt and Isaac laughing like old friends.

"Sela, please come in," Hoyt beckons.

Isaac stands.

"I'm sorry I'm late," I say as I join them.

Hoyt looks down at his watch. "You're right on time."

Right on time is late for me. I'm the person who always arrives early. I'm not a fan of rushing, and I don't like feeling unprepared. I like to take my time, stop for coffee, and chat with folks as I stroll into the office.

I look around, flustered.

"No Cobie this morning?" I ask.

"She decided she wanted to stay at the inn and help Trixie and Willa bake and gut pumpkins for tonight's ginger pumpkin pie and toasted pumpkin seeds. So, it'll be just you and me on today's adventure," Isaac explains.

Darn, I wanted to take her to the ice rink and park today.

My disappointment must show on my face.

"It was a hard choice for her. She wanted to see you again, but she's never made pies before," he consoles.

"Thankfully, I'll get to see her tomorrow night to hunt elves, right?"

He smiles. "There's no way she'll miss that."

"So, what is on today's agenda?" Isaac asks.

My stomach lets out a loud growl, and he lifts an eyebrow in question.

"First stop is for food. I missed breakfast this morning," I reply.

He opens the door to town hall and motions for me to lead the way.

The Snow Bird Café is only two doors down from town hall, so we duck in and slide into a corner booth.

Joe Walsh, the owner of the café, waves to us from the kitchen.

"What can I get you, Sela?" he calls.

"Sausage egg and cheese on a bun and ..." I reply and then lift an eyebrow to Isaac.

"I'm still stuffed with Alice's biscuits and gravy."

"Coffee?" I ask.

He nods.

"And two coffees please, Joe," I bellow.

Joe gives us a thumbs-up.

Isaac's assessing eyes glide across the café, decorated with paper snowflakes that hang from the ceiling by clear fishing lines. Snowmen and women line the counter. A Fraser fir—with gorgeous hand-painted wooden cardinals, robins, woodpeckers, snow buntings, and tufted tit-mouse dangling from its branches—sits by the door. It's wrapped with snowball garland and tossed with iridescent white tinsel.

He reaches for the camera bag at his side and looks at me. "Do you mind?"

I shake my head. "Not at all."

He stands to his feet, pulls the camera from its containment, and begins to walk around the room.

He focuses on Joe through the window into the kitchen as he flips pancakes, then moves to a couple sitting on the stools by the counter, enjoying their breakfast.

He snaps the tree as Joe makes it to our table with a pot of coffee and fills our cups. I take hold of the sugar bowl on the table, add two cubes to my cup, followed by a glug of cream from the small pitcher, and stir.

Isaac turns his lens to me as I close my eyes, blow the surface, and take the first sip.

When I open my eyes, his camera is still focused on me as he walks a circle around our booth.

I grin at him. Turn my head to look out the window. Pull my hair to the side to cover my face. But no matter how I attempt to hide, he just continues to shoot.

Joe returns with a plate and leans over and takes a look at Isaac's screen.

He smiles and nods as he sets the food in front of me.

"Stunning," he quips on a wink.

I can feel the heat rising in my cheeks.

I glance up at Isaac. "Sit, please," I demand.

He puts the camera away and parks himself across from me.

"So, you and Cobie's mom are divorced?" I ask, attempting to make small talk as I dig into my meal.

"We are. Have been for five years now," he says.

"She seems well adjusted," I observe.

He leans back against the red faux leather bench and sighs. "That's all Lonnie. She's a great mother," he praises.

"But not a great wife?" I regret the words as soon as they leave my tongue.

"It wasn't that. We met at the University of Texas. We married young, right out of college. I had my fine arts degree, and she had a nursing degree. We had so many plans. I wanted to see the world, and she wanted a family. We compromised and decided that she'd take a position as a travel nurse for five years and I'd pick up photography gigs wherever her job took us. We were excited, both of us, and it worked for about a year. Then, one surprise pregnancy later, and we were back in Texas, living in her parents' basement."

"And you weren't happy about that?" I guess.

His forehead creases as he chooses his words.

"I was happy about the baby, but not the timing exactly. I had just started booking real jobs and wanted to get my foothold in the industry, save some money, buy a house, and then fill it with babies. Having to stay with the in-laws while Lonnie worked nights in the ER and I took jobs shooting middle school pictures was not the way I wanted to start our family."

"You made God laugh," I muse.

His brows go up.

"My mom always told Brannigan and me that if we wanted to make God laugh, all we had to do was tell him our plans," I explain.

He nods as he takes a pull from his mug and then continues, "That's so true. We scrimped and saved every dime and stayed with her folks until Cobie came. Then, we rented a two-bedroom apartment closer to the hospital."

"Still not your dream?"

He shakes his head. "Cobie had me wrapped around her finger from the moment she took her first breath, and all I wanted was to give my girls the world. So, when *Epic Odysseys* offered me a hefty contract, I jumped at the chance. It was my dream job, and it was going to afford me the ability to provide for us in the way I wanted. Cobie was two at the time, and I knew I'd have to travel, but I don't think Lonnie or I realized how spending large chucks of time away from each other would affect us. We grew apart. She was content working and living around the corner from where she had grown up. She became a homebody, and I became addicted to the thrill of wanderlust."

"That's sad," I mutter.

"A little, but we split before we began to resent one another, and that allowed us to stay friends. She met Greg, an oncologist, two years ago, and they married last summer. He's a good guy, and he treats Cobie well. That's all I could ask for," he asserts.

"What about you? No new woman in your life?"

Why did I ask that?

His lips lift in a half-smile. "No one special. How about you?"

"Nope. Norah signed me up for a dating app last week, and it's made some matches, but I haven't had the courage to respond yet."

"I bet you've had a flood of messages," he muses, and my stomach does a little flip.

"I did have a boyfriend back in Boise, but we broke it off before graduation. He intended to stay in the city, and I couldn't wait to get back to Lake Mistletoe." I continue ignoring the electric pulse in the air.

"So, you're a homebody as well," he notes.

"Not really. I mean, I obviously love it here, but I'm not content working and sitting at home, twiddling my thumbs. I want to go everywhere. I want to see the places that I've only read about in books or seen in movies. To taste exotic foods and experience new cultures, dip my toes in the Mediterranean Sea, sunbathe on the deck of a yacht in the South of France. All of those things, but when I lay my head down at home, I want it to be here. Home is where your people are. It's where you find peace and solace. It's the soft place you land after spreading your wings."

He takes a deep breath and blows it out slowly. "I don't think I've ever felt that way about a place. I'm an Army brat, so we moved around a lot when I was a kid, never putting any roots down. San Antonio is Lonnie's hometown, and it's where Cobie is. Being with her is the closest thing I have to solace. Even if it's only a day or two spent in my ex-wife's pool house between assignments."

The look of sadness on his face causes me to reach across the table and place my hand over his.

His eyes flicker from mine to where our hands rest as Joe appears.

I quickly pull my arm back to my side as Joe places the ticket on the table.

"You two look like you're having a deep conversation," Joe muses.

"She's pulling all of my secrets out of me," Isaac says.

Joe chuckles. "A pretty woman can do that. You'd better be careful."

Joe winks at me as he takes my empty plate.

"Can I get you guys anything else?" he asks.

"I'm stuffed, and we have a lot to see," I answer.

I pull a twenty from my wallet and lay it on top of the ticket as I stand. Joe gives me a peck on the cheek as I tug my coat back on. Then, he shakes Isaac's hand.

"Remember what I said. Watch out for that one."

"Yes, sir," Isaac replies.

I roll my eyes as he opens the door, and we continue our adventure.

Chapter Seven

Isaac

WHILE COBIE TELLS ME ALL ABOUT HER DAY OF BAKING WITH Trixie and Willa, I spend the evening downloading the hundreds of photos I've captured over the last three days. Each sequence tells a story of the enchanting life in Lake Mistletoe.

Sela and I spent the afternoon strolling the streets of the city and talking to every person we passed by. Each one with a unique perspective of what makes this town so magical.

I made a ton of mental notes to share with Dawn before I leave.

My favorite shots of the day are of Sela in the café, Sela showing me her skating skills at the ice rink, and Sela posing with a snowman—dressed in an overcoat and wire-framed glasses with a bright red leash in his tree-branch hand, attached to a snowy four-legged friend.

I laugh at her expression as she takes in the perfectly sculpted bulldog with a black button nose.

"What's so funny, Daddy?" Cobie asks, climbing down from the bed and into my lap in front of the computer.

"I think Sela made a friend today," I tell her as I point out the frame.

"Is that a puppy?" she squeals.

"Yep. A snow pup."

"Can we make one?" she asks.

"I don't think I'm that artistically inclined, but we can build a snowman before we leave if you want."

"Yes! I'll ask Miss Alice for a carrot, and it can wear one of my scarves and my mittens."

I look down at her, and it hits me that I've never played in the snow with my daughter. Not once in her eight years of life.

I swallow back the emotion and make her a promise. "We'll build a snowman, make snow angels, and challenge Keller to a snowball fight."

Her eyes light up. "Can Lexie play too?"

"If it's okay with her parents," I agree, and Cobie jumps down and runs to tell her new friend of our plans.

My phone chimes, and I pick it up and wake the screen.

It's a text from Dawn, informing me that her husband's band got a gig playing at the Sun Valley Resort Hotel tomorrow so they flew in a couple of days early and would be arriving at the inn before dinner.

I tap out a reply and go in search of Cobie.

"We're here!"

I look up from my plate of confections to see my coworker Dawn Taylor and her husband, Daniel, standing in the doorway of the great room.

Dawn and I both joined the creative team at *Epic Odysseys* around the same time. She had come over from an online fashion magazine under the same imprint that went dark.

Fashion and gossip are her wheelhouse, but as soon as she started getting paid to travel to five-star resorts, exotic regions, and cozy, romantic locations, she fell in love with the world of travel journalism.

Dawn's short blonde bob is hidden under a wool cap that matches her cashmere turtleneck. Daniel is in a dark gray henley, topped by a black jean jacket. A guitar case in one hand and the handle of a large suitcase in the other.

"Glad you guys made it safe and sound," I say.

The temperature dropped below freezing, the snowfall turned to ice, and the wind kicked up about an hour ago, making for treacherous road conditions.

"We rented a beast of a truck. Luckily, Daniel here can drive just about anything with wheels."

"That'll come in handy here," I quip.

"What are you doing?" Dawn asks as she looks around the room.

I sit, surrounded by an array of colorful icing, sprinkles, and freshly baked Christmas cookies.

"Decorating cookies for Santa's elves," Cobie answers.

After dinner, we, along with Willa and a group of other guests, embarked on a delightful mess-making adventure, determined to create the most festive and delicious cookies. Trixie is tasked with picking the ones she thinks Santa would like best at the end of the night.

"Santa? Isn't it a bit early for the big guy?" Dawn asks.

"Miss Trixie is going to leave them out for the elves that come tomorrow night. They'll take them back to Santa," Cobie explains.

"Elves?"

"Yep. They come to hide treats and mistletoe for Santa, and we get to look for them with candles," Cobie exclaims.

"Really? Can I get in on that action?" Dawn asks.

Cobie's eyes go to her and narrow. "I can ask Miss Sela if you can come, too, but you'll have to help make cookies."

Dawn's eyes come to me. "Miss Sela?"

"She's our new friend," Cobie answers before I get the chance.

Dawn raises an eyebrow. "Is that right?"

Cobie nods. "Yep. She's nice. I think she'll say yes, but you need to change. You don't wanna get icing on your fancy clothes."

Dawn glances down at herself. "You're right, kid. I'll be back," she says before hurrying off.

Daniel throws his hand up in greeting as he follows.

"All right, Cobie," I say, rolling up my sleeves, "let's turn these plain cookies into works of art!"

I hand her a piping bag filled with vibrant icing, showing her how to create intricate designs.

Cobie watches intently, her small fingers gripping the piping bag with determination.

With an unsteady hand, she covers the stockings and sweaters with red royal icing. Her face lights up with joy every time she successfully completes a cookie and sets it on the platter with mine.

However, our artistic endeavor quickly takes a messy turn when I accidentally squeeze the icing bag too hard, causing a glob of green icing to splatter across the table.

Cobie gasps, her eyes wide with surprise. "You're making a mess, Daddy."

I hold up one of my creations; it's a delightful disaster with uneven lines and smeared colors. "What do you mean? This is a masterpiece."

She giggles and shakes her head.

Dawn returns, wearing an oversize T-shirt and black sweatpants, and takes a seat at our table.

"Where's Daniel?" I ask.

"He's unpacking us and taking a nap," she says as she squeezes a dollop of green icing on a plate and grabs a cookie shaped like a wreath.

"A nap? It's almost bedtime," Cobie points out.

"He's a night owl. Rock 'n' roll does that to you, kid," Dawn replies.

Cobie scrunches up her nose. "Rock 'n' roll."

Dawn taps her chin. "You can scowl all you want, but one day, your teenage self will be drooling over a hot guitar player too."

Cobie's eyes go round. "Ew, no, boys are gross, and so is drooling."

Dawn laughs.

We continue to work until we've finished frosting two dozen cookies.

Cobie inspects each of our platters.

"What do you think?" Dawn asks.

"Yours are really pretty," Cobie praises.

"Well, how'd I do?" I ask.

Cobie twists her lips.

"They're good," she chirps.

"Good, huh? But not as good as your mom's?"

She shrugs. "Not quite. But all you need is some practice. We can make another batch tomorrow."

I lean over and whisper in her ear, "You know where we can get amazing cookies? Paris. The shop in the lobby of our hotel sells perfect macarons."

"Yeah, you said," she mumbles.

"You're going to love them," I continue.

"I know. Can I show my cookies to Miss Trixie now?"

I stand and reach for my camera.

"Let's get a few pictures of them first. You get beside Miss Dawn and hold up your creations for me."

She climbs up in the seat, and Dawn scoots her chair closer. She hands Cobie one of the platters, and she takes the other.

They smile their widest smiles as I take photos of them, being sure to focus on the sticky fingers and color-smeared faces and Cobie's delight as she bites into one of the reindeer's antlers.

I tousle her hair affectionately. "We make a great team, don't we?"

Cobie nods, and she beams. "Best team ever, Daddy!"

Trixie makes a round to all the tables and praises each child for their decorating skills before announcing that she can't choose a favorite so she's going to take a cookie from each child for Santa. "He's going to love them all."

"How will he know which one is from me?" Lexie asks.

Trixie gives her a wink. "Santa knows all. He'll be able to taste the difference."

I snap a picture of the tears of excitement as they leak down the little girl's cheeks before lowering my camera and taking in this messy, laughter-filled room and the wonder on Cobie's face, and I realize that it's not just about the cookies for the kids.

They—no, we—created memories that will last a lifetime.

Chapter Eight

Sela

I MEET HANNAH AND NORAH AT THE FLOWER SHOP AT LUNCH. THE two of them are choosing the flowers for Willa's baby shower, and I'm here for moral support and Hannah's hash brown casserole.

They settle on a mix of freesias, delphiniums, and irises that Norah arranges with dried pampas grass and orange and green feathers.

"I like it. It's whimsical, and it will match the table runners and the balloon arches I ordered," Hannah chirps.

"Perfect. I'll get an order in for twelve and a larger version for the gift table," Norah says.

"Great. Now, let's eat," Hannah suggests.

We follow her into the back, where Norah has a small break area, and she pulls three Tupperware containers filled with the cheesy potato goodness.

"So, Sela, have you swiped right on any men yet?" Norah asks as she fishes plastic forks from a drawer under the microwave.

"Nope."

"Why not?" Hannah asks.

I shrug. "No one has piqued my interest."

"No one, except for a handsome photographer, you mean?" Norah pokes.

"My interest in Isaac is strictly professional," I inform her as I dig into my meal.

"Oh, come on. That man is so fine," Norah says.

"He's also leaving in a couple of days," I remind her.

"So? He's here now," Hannah interjects.

My eyes slide to her. "Yes, with his eight-year-old daughter."

"Who is more than happy spending time underfoot with Mom and Alice in the kitchen. You should climb that man like a tree while they have her distracted," Norah adds.

"You're crazy," I scoff.

Hannah shrugs. "Nothing wrong with a little Christmas fling."

Norah raises her fork in the air and points at her. "Exactly. I encouraged both you and Willa to have a holiday affair."

"Look how well that worked out. We both ended up packing up and moving to Idaho," Hannah quips.

"You're welcome," Norah bellows.

"Slow your roll, ladies. Nobody is looking to move anywhere," I command.

Norah grins. "That's the beauty of it. You already live here, Sela. No risk of upheaving your life. Just upheaving your nether regions." She waggles her eyebrows.

I shake my head. "Like I said, even if he were interested—which he is not—he leaves in two days. I think my nether regions are safe."

"You mean sad," Norah mutters.

She's not wrong.

I spend the rest of the afternoon catching up on work that I set aside the past few days, and I only come up for air when I hear the sweetest, spirited voice calling my name from the front of the building.

I stand and pop my head out of my office door and peer down the corridor to see Isaac, Cobie, and a tall blonde I don't recognize gathered around Roxie's desk.

Cobie spots me and raises a large black flashlight. "Sela! We're ready to hunt Santa's elves," she squeals.

I place my hands on my hips and march down the hall to meet her. "And what is that?" I ask.

"It's a flashlight. Daddy says I'm too little to carry a candle around so I have to use this instead," she explains.

I grin at her as she bounces on the toes of her white fur-lined boots.

"Roxie and I thought about that, too, and I stopped by the hardware store this morning and got you a surprise," I tell her.

Her eyes widen. "A surprise?"

Roxie leans over her desk and hands me the paper bag. Tucked inside are battery-operated LED candlesticks in brass settings with a handle.

I pull one out and click the power button on the bottom.

The candle glows to life and flickers like a true flame.

Cobie's eyes light up as she sets the flashlight on the corner of the desk and takes the handle with her mitten-covered fingers.

"Yay! Thank you," she exclaims.

I ruffle the curls at the top of her head. "You're very welcome."

I stand and greet Isaac and their guest.

"Sela, this is Dawn Taylor. She's the journalist who will be writing the story about Lake Mistletoe for *Epic Odysseys*."

The girl smiles brightly.

"It's nice to meet you," I greet as a sliver of jealousy slides through me at the sight of her arm in Isaac's elbow.

"You too. I hope you don't mind that I'm tagging along tonight," Dawn states warmly.

I shake myself from my ridiculous reaction and return her smile. "Not at all. I just finished up, and I'm going to change into something more comfortable. If you guys can give me ten minutes, I'll be right back," I reply.

"Take your time," Isaac prompts.

I hurry back to my office and grab my tote, then make my way to the ladies' room to change.

I slip into a pair of fleece-lined camel-colored leggings; a warm, oversized, off-shoulder brown sweater; and thick, fuzzy socks. Then, I tug on a pair of tall dark brown duck boots and pull the laces tight.

Grabbing my rust-hued felt fedora and tossing it on my head, I wrap my neck with a thick cream-colored scarf my mother knit for me and tuck the matching gloves in my crossbody.

I throw my pantsuit and heels into the tote, drop it off on my desk, and lock up.

As we stroll down the sidewalk, Isaac tells us a story of the nisse, which are festive gnomes with long white beards that travel on a yule goat on Christmas Eve, knocking on the doors of homes in Denmark and passing out presents. Boys and girls leave a bowl of warm oatmeal, topped with butter, for the nisse as a show of gratitude.

"So, they don't leave cookies and milk for Santa?" Cobie asks.

"The nisse are Santa's helpers in Denmark, and they prefer porridge," Isaac explains.

"Like elves?" Cobie asks.

"Yes. Like elves. Maybe one day, we can spend Christmas in Copenhagen and see the nisse," he says.

Cobie frowns. "I like cookies better than oatmeal, Daddy."

He chuckles. "That's not the point. It's experiencing the new traditions. Every country has its own way of celebrating the holidays. Like this year, we'll go to midnight mass with friends of mine in Paris, and then we'll sit for the *Le Réveillon* feast of oysters and foie gras and yule log cake. Then, we'll wait for *Père Noël*, who we call Santa Claus, to come and bring the presents."

Her nose wrinkles. "What's foy grot?"

"Foie gras. It's goose liver, a French delicacy."

"Liver? Yuck!"

He chuckles. "It's quite good, rich and buttery, with a delicious gravy."

"I like our way of celebrating," she mutters.

Me too. I'll take turkey and stuffing over oysters and goose liver any day.

The four of us meet the rest of the revelers at the park that leads to the south side of the lake.

The townspeople, bundled in scarves and warm outerwear, cheerfully greet us as we join the gathered crowd.

Their laughter mingles with the gentle lapping of the lake against the shore.

"Sela," my mother calls, "we've been waiting for you!"

I lead Isaac, Cobie, and Dawn to the table at our right, where my mother and Trixie are handing out candles.

"Hi, Mom," I say as we approach.

"Hi, kiddo. Who do you have here?" Mom asks.

"This is Isaac Ralston and his daughter, Cobie, and this is Dawn Taylor. Isaac and Dawn work for a travel magazine, and I brought them here to experience the hunt. Guys, this is my mother, Linden Prince," I introduce.

Mom gives them a brilliant smile. "Welcome to Lake Mistletoe. It's lovely to meet you all."

"Likewise," Isaac returns.

Mom's eyes dart down to Cobie. "Are you ready to find the elves and their gifts?"

Cobie nods enthusiastically.

Mom reaches behind her to pluck candles from a basket.

"I have my own," Cobie informs her as she passes the others to us.

"Perfect. Now, remember to walk lightly and to talk softly. The elves are fast and nimble. If you see a green bag or box with a red bow, it will contain a surprise. And there will be mistletoe hanging somewhere close," Mom explains. Then, she leans down to Cobie and whispers, "Let the magic guide you."

With a sense of wonder, we join the procession as Mayor Miller guides us onto the path that encompasses the lake, our candles casting dancing shadows on the snow-covered ground.

The night is alive with the soft whispers of the frosty wind and the occasional hoot of a snowy owl hiding in the nearby trees.

As we walk, everyone begins to break off and dart in different directions as they catch sight of bags hanging from branches and boxes tucked behind rocks.

Isaac, with his trusty camera strapped at his side, pulls it from the bag and begins to capture images of children running ahead of their parents and searching behind trees for Santa's little helpers, fathers with their hands full of found treasures, and delighted mothers whose faces are aglow with candlelight.

"This is something else," Dawn murmurs beside me. "I wish Daniel were here to see this."

"Daniel?" I question.

"My husband. His band is playing at the ski resort tonight. Isaac and I are going over to watch them later tonight. You should join us," she invites.

Her husband.

An inexplicable relief washes over me.

"I might do that," I agree.

Cobie spots a box standing on top of one of the pedestrian bridge railings and beckons Isaac.

He passes his camera off to Dawn, and she aims it in their direction as he lifts Cobie off her feet and holds her steady as she reaches out to clasp the prize.

"Sela, come look," Cobie cries, and I hurry to their side.

She plucks the top from the box and finds a nutcracker ornament that has *Lake Mistletoe* carved into the base, along with a hardcover copy of *The Nutcracker* picture book by E.T.A. Hoffmann.

"Wow," she gasps.

"*The Nutcracker*. Your favorite. How did the elves know?" Isaac muses.

"Christmas magic," Cobie whispers.

"It must be," he agrees.

Dawn calls our attention, and the three of us pose with the book and ornament. She snaps a picture, and then her eyes focus above us.

"Oh my, look what I spy," she says as she points to the lamppost above us.

Our eyes follow, and tied to the top with a silk ribbon is a sprig of greenery with tiny white berries.

"It's mistletoe," Cobie squeals.

She wraps an arm around each of our necks and kisses our cheeks.

"Now, you two kiss," she prompts.

"Yeah, you two kiss," Dawn calls as she raises the camera.

I can feel the blood rush to my cheeks as Cobie looks at us expectantly.

Isaac's free hand comes to the side of my face, a mischievous glint in his eyes as he bends to place a quick, soft kiss on my lips. Lingering for just a brief moment. My breath catches at the contact as the air around us fills with the click of the camera and the giggles of a thrilled eight-year-old.

"That was hot," Dawn mutters as she looks at the camera screen.

Isaac takes a step back and plants Cobie on her feet. Then, his eyes turn to me, and he opens his mouth to say something, but before the words leave his lips, Cobie shrieks and points to the other side of the bridge.

"An elf!"

She takes off in a sprint toward the costumed figure that disappears into the tree line.

"Did you see him, Daddy?" she asks as we catch up to her.

"I did."

"Look, he left another treat," Dawn points out.

Cobie picks it up and starts to tear into it just as a little girl in a puffy jacket trots up to us, an older woman on her heels.

"Oops, someone beat us to it," the lady says as she grasps the girl's hand.

Cobie looks down at the bag and back to the girl, who doesn't have a bag of boxes yet. Cobie smiles and extends the gift to her.

"I was just getting it for you. I think you saw it first," she says.

The other child's expression brightens as she takes the offered bag.

"You don't have to do that—" the woman begins.

Cobie interrupts, "It's for her. From Santa Claus."

The girl opens the bag and finds a stuffed calico kitten inside. "Look, Grammy. It's Ralphie," the girl cries.

Her grandmother's eyes begin to water. "It sure is," she whispers.

Then, she looks up at Isaac, who has taken the camera back over, the lens taking in the girl's delight.

"Her kitty got out of the house on Thanksgiving and was struck by a car."

The child hugs the stuffed animal to her chest as Cobie lays a hand on her shoulder.

"See? Santa sent it just for you."

Dawn sniffles as the two of them continue across the bridge. "Man, those elves are good."

Isaac looks down at his daughter, who is holding her candle in one hand and her book in the other with pride.

"They are something else. The joy they bring to Lake Mistletoe every winter is epic," I agree.

We reach a clearing, where the moonlight shimmers across the misty lake. Isaac and Dawn make their way to the perfect spot to snap the scene while Cobie and I head to one of the benches that dot the lakeshore.

Chapter Nine

Sela

COBIE SETTLES IN BESIDE AN ELDERLY GENTLEMAN WITH A SHORT white beard who is watching the festivities. He is wearing a red-and-black plaid newsboy cap and a pair of worn-out black corduroy slacks, held up over his white thermal shirt by a pair of red suspenders.

"Hi," she greets the man.

"Hello to you," he returns.

"I'm Cobie."

"It's nice to meet you, Cobie. I'm Kris."

She gestures to me. "This is my new friend, Sela. She kissed my daddy under the mistletoe."

His eyes go wide. "A Christmas kiss. That's a true gift," he bellows.

She beams as she drops the candle at her feet and holds up her book and nutcracker. "And look what I found. Santa sent it to me with one of his elves. He knows I like *The Nutcracker*. Mom said if I work really hard in dance class, one day, I might get to play Clara in the ballet."

"Well, isn't that something? Are you going to see *The Nutcracker* over at the resort next week?" he asks.

"Where?"

"Up on top of the mountain at Sun Valley. They are showing the New York City Ballet rendition on the big screen in the theater room."

Excitement lights her eyes before it quickly flickers out. "We won't be here next week. My daddy and I are going to France."

"You don't sound very excited about that," he notes.

She shrugs. "He has to work in France, so we're going to spend Christmas there."

"I don't think he's working," I interrupt.

She looks at me. "He's not?"

"No, he told me he was taking the holidays off this year to spend them with you," I tell her.

Her forehead creases. "Then, why are we going to Paris?" she asks.

"Your dad would have to answer that, but I think he wants to take you because he thinks you'll love it," I reply.

"It's a great city with lots of lights and history," Kris tells her.

"You've been?" she asks.

"Oh, yes, I go all the time. It's very beautiful," he muses.

"Lake Mistletoe is beautiful," she states.

"Yes, it is," he agrees.

"Do you think Santa will be able to find me in Paris?" she asks him.

He smiles at her. "Santa can find you no matter where you are. He has Christmas magic to guide him, remember?"

She sighs. "I guess."

"You sound skeptical."

"What if I've been good all year, but I do something bad before Christmas? Do you think Santa will forgive me?" she whispers to him.

"Oh, Santa is a very forgiving guy. He looks at the heart of a person," Kris explains.

"I hope so," she mutters.

"You know, Cobie, I think you will have a wonderful Christmas this year. It doesn't matter where you spend it as long as you and your father are together. So, you should just enjoy your time in Lake

Mistletoe and not worry about tomorrow. Everything will work out just like it's supposed to."

Isaac and Dawn find their way to us, and Cobie introduces them to Kris.

"I think it's time to head back to the inn. Sorry we didn't catch an elf and get a picture," Isaac tells his daughter.

"That's okay. I'll remember him," Cobie chirps.

She goes up on her knees and cups her mouth to whisper into Kris's ear.

He nods.

Then, she hops off the bench, gathers her candle and treats, and hands them to me before taking Isaac's hand.

As we make our way down the path that leads back to the park, Kris calls after us, "Cobie!"

We pause, and she looks over her shoulder at him.

"Santa knows all our secrets, even the ones we keep hidden under our beds."

Her eyes go round as he turns back to the lake.

"What was that all about?" Dawn asks.

I shrug.

"Do you know him?" Isaac asks me.

I shake my head. "Nope. He must be visiting too," I say.

Although he does look vaguely familiar.

Must be a return tourist.

We run into Norah and Sammy at Mom and Trixie's table, and Dawn talks them into coming out to see her husband perform. Trixie offers to take Cobie back to the inn so Isaac and I can go as well.

Isaac bends a knee and speaks to his girl. "Are you sure it's okay if Miss Trixie takes you back?"

"I'm sure. We're gonna help Willa string popcorn for the Christmas tree," she exclaims.

"That sounds fun." He kisses her forehead. "I promise not to be too late so I can tuck you in, and we'll read your new book tonight."

She kisses his chin, and he stands as she joins Mom and Trixie behind the table and helps them load the baskets with candles as they are returned.

Sammy runs ahead of us to fetch the Jeep while the rest of us pop into the market so Dawn can use the restroom.

We grab a couple of bottles of water and a large bag of Cheetos and get into line.

Norah picks up a copy of *Country Weekly Magazine* and sighs.

"Garrett Tuttle is getting married this Christmas. There goes another dream ripped from my bucket list," she quips.

"Garrett Tuttle is on your bucket list? But you're married," I tell her, which is something she already knows, just as Dawn rejoins us.

"He's one of my hall passes too. I'm a sucker for a man in tight jeans who can play a guitar," Dawn agrees.

"And he's not even marrying another singer or actress or model. He's marrying his high school sweetheart that he reconnected with on a trip home." I swoon.

Dawn rolls her eyes. "That only happens in Hallmark movies and romance novels."

I pluck the magazine from Norah's fingers and turn it to Dawn. "Or in Balsam Ridge, Tennessee."

Isaac laughs as he pays for our refreshments. "Come on, you crazy women. Let's go so you can ogle some musicians in real life," he says as he leads us out of the store.

"And Dawn here gets to take one of them home with her," Norah sings, and then she stops and looks over her shoulder. "Are any of his bandmates single?"

I groan.

"As a matter of fact, Les, the lead singer, is a certified bachelor," Dawn answers.

Norah wags her eyebrows at me. "Ooh, did your nether regions hear that?" she asks under her breath.

I stick my tongue out at her.

Chapter Ten

Isaac

WE'RE LED TO A RESERVED TABLE IN FRONT OF THE STAGE, where Daniel's band is already entertaining the patrons. A server comes by, and we order a round of cocktails and some appetizers.

Sela looks down at her phone and then leans over to Norah. "Bran and Hannah are in the parking lot. I texted them from the park to see if they wanted to meet us here."

"Great! Hey, Isaac, can you ask the server to add another cranberry martini and a Guinness to our order?" Norah asks.

I do as she requested and run into Bran and his girlfriend at the bar. I show them to our table, and Bran helps Hannah remove her coat as she settles in next to Sela.

Sela introduces Dawn to the couple and points out Daniel on the guitar.

The server returns with our order, and Bran joins me and Sammy as we watch the girls enjoy their pretty red drinks, which apparently go down smooth because they are flagging down the guy again in a matter of minutes to order seconds.

"It's going to be one of those kinda nights," Sammy says.

"Yep," Bran agrees.

"What kinda night is that?" I ask.

They slide their eyes to me.

"The fun kind," Bran says as he slaps me on the back.

"Another round, fellas?" our server, Kerr, asks.

"Not for me. I have to drive," Sammy says.

"And I have to play Joseph tomorrow afternoon," Bran says as he shakes his head.

"And I have to read to Cobie when we get home," I agree.

Kerr looks over at the girls, who are now standing at the foot of the stage. "For them?"

"Yeah, why not? Let them have their fun," Bran says.

We sit back and watch the females drink and dance and cut loose.

"Sammy, Dad and I could use an extra pair of hands to help get our boat parade entry ready for next weekend," Bran says.

Sammy shakes his head. "Nah, man. Bob and Keller would roast me if I helped you guys."

"Come on. They have more than enough help," Bran points out.

"I know, but you're talking about my father- and brother-in-law. You know how serious they take that contest," Sammy defends.

"Hannah is Norah's cousin, and that makes her your cousin-in-law. I plan to put a ring on her finger this Christmas, so that makes us practically related," Bran explains.

"You're reaching," Sammy grunts.

"Fine," Bran spits and turns his attention to me. "How about you? Want to help me bring down the mighty Harrises this year?"

"Sorry, man. I'm leaving the day after tomorrow," I remind him.

"Damn, that's right."

"I'd love to come by and photograph your progress before I go though."

"Sure. Stop by Smitten in Lake Mistletoe Event Services sometime after the nativity tomorrow."

"Smitten in Lake Mistletoe?" I ask.

"It's Hannah's business. She has space in the back, and that's where we've been working on it. I don't have anywhere at the tree house, and I can't trust Keller to keep his hands and eyes to himself at our shop," he clarifies.

"Tree house?" I query.

"Yep. My house is built up among the pines and foliage on the side of the mountain. It's a grown man's tree house," he elaborates.

"Gotcha."

"Wait, did you say you're proposing?" Sammy circles back.

"Yep. I picked the ring up this morning. Her mom is coming in on Christmas Eve, and I plan to pop the question then," Bran answers.

"Congratulations!" Sammy barks.

Bran brings a finger to his lips.

"Sorry," Sammy mumbles.

Daniel tugs Dawn onstage as the music slows.

Bran stands. "That's our cue, fellas," he says. He makes his way through the crowd that's gathered on the floor and takes Hannah by the hand, pulling her into his arms.

Sammy's eyes slide to mine. "What do you say? Let's go spin those girls around the dance floor," he prompts.

The two of us wade our way to the front, where Norah and Sela are leaning against the edge, staring up at the lead singer as he croons into the microphone.

Sammy walks up to Norah's back and wraps his arms around

her as he whispers into her ear. I approach Sela and tap her on the shoulder.

She glances back at me.

"May I have this dance?" I ask, spreading my arms wide.

She turns and walks into me. My hands fall to her hips, and we begin to sway to the music.

She is light as a feather. I pick her up off her feet and twirl her while she laughs.

When I set her back down, I take her elbow and pull her in until we are nose to nose.

Her eyes flit to my mouth, and she licks her bottom lip.

Unable to stop myself, I lean forward and touch my lips to hers.

She gasps in surprise, and I take the opportunity to deepen the kiss.

Her eyes flutter closed, and she presses her chest into mine as her arms go around my neck. I feed a hand under her hair at her ear and hold her face as our tongues tangle in a delicious dance of their own.

Every cell in my body is firing on all cylinders, and I get lost in the moment until the music ends and the band begins the intro to another song.

Sela's hold on me releases, and her hand slides to clutch my wrist as her eyes open.

I rest my forehead against hers.

"You taste like cranberries," she murmurs.

"I think that's you," I tell her.

She bears back and blinks up at me. "What was that?" she asks breathlessly.

My finger slides to her chin and lifts her face, guiding her gaze above us, where a kissing ball is hanging from the ceiling.

Her mouth falls open, and then her eyes snap back to mine and narrow. "Did you lead me under the mistletoe again on purpose?" she asks.

I smile. "Happy accident."

"Happy?" she questions.

"It gave me a chance to kiss you properly. That one at the lake was not my best work," I mutter.

"I thought it was nice," she states.

"Exactly my point," I reply.

"We did have an audience," she says.

I lean back and look around.

Bran, Hannah, Sammy, Norah, and Dawn have all returned to our table, and their eyes are focused on us.

"I think we still do," I tell her.

She follows my motion and turns in their direction.

"Wonderful," she mutters.

I take her hand, and our fingers entwine as I lead her back to her friends.

"The other kiss was hot, but that last one was an inferno," Dawn says.

"What other kiss?" Norah asks.

Sela blushes as we take our seats.

"Honey, don't pry," Sammy coaxes.

She turns in her seat to face him. "Hello. Have we met?"

He grins and taps her on the nose.

"It's getting late. You can interrogate her tomorrow," he promises.

As if on cue, Norah lets out a long yawn.

"Okay, take me home, lover." She gives in as she wraps her arms around his shoulders.

He chuckles as he stands, bringing her to her unsteady feet.

"Sela? You ready?" he asks as he urges his wife in the direction of the door.

"Yeah." She turns to me and asks tentatively, "Do you want to come to my apartment for a nightcap?"

It physically pains me to decline the offer.

"I promised Cobie I'd be back to tuck her in and read to her," I inform her.

"Oh, right. Of course," she says rapidly as she stands.

I catch her elbow. "If it wasn't for that," I say.

She smiles. "Yeah."

I let her go, and she follows after Norah and Sammy.

"Isaac, you need a ride back to the inn?" Sammy asks.

"He can ride with me and Daniel," Dawn offers.

"Cool. See you guys tomorrow," he says, guiding Norah and Sela, who have locked arms, to the exit.

"I think we need to head out too. Mary and Joseph need their beauty sleep," Bran declares.

He and Hannah say their good-byes, leaving Dawn and me to wait while Daniel and his bandmates break down their equipment.

She slides her chair closer to mine. "You're in trouble," she sings.

Yes, I am.

Once everything is loaded into the truck, Daniel drives us to the inn, where Trixie and a sleepy Cobie are curled up on the couch, watching *Rudolph*.

I thank Trixie for spending the evening with her before I scoop her up into my arms and carry her upstairs.

"Did you have a good night?" I ask as I lay her in bed and pull the covers up to her chin.

She nods. "We made popcorn and cranberry strings for the big tree, and then we ate the leftovers while we watched cartoons."

"That sounds like a lot of fun," I tell her.

"What about you, Daddy? Did you and Sela have fun?" she asks.

I pick *The Nutcracker* book up from the nightstand and lie down on the bed beside her. "We did. We danced while Daniel and his friends played music."

"Is she a good dancer?"

"Yep. Almost as good as me," I tease.

She giggles.

I open the book.

She curls into my side and lays her head on my chest as I begin to read. She makes it halfway through the story before she loses the fight and falls fast asleep.

I click off the lamp, join her, and dream of mistletoe.

87

Chapter Eleven

Isaac

COBIE AND I AWAKEN TO A SWEET AROMA AND FIND HAL IN THE kitchen, flipping thick slices of bread on a griddle.

"Good morning, early risers. Are you guys hungry?" he asks as Cobie hops up onto one of the barstools.

"I am! What are you making?" she asks.

"French toast and sausage links," he answers.

"Yum."

I ask Hal if it'd be all right for me to use the kitchen tonight to make a Swedish Christmas dessert for everyone, and he gives me his permission.

"Alice will be upset if you don't incorporate gingerbread," he warns.

"Not sure how to do that," I admit.

He slaps me on the back as he slides a plate in front of me. "I've got you covered. I'll whip up a batch of gingerbread eggnog to serve with your dessert."

"I appreciate that."

Cobie digs into her breakfast, eager to finish.

Once her plate is cleaned, she runs off to get dressed and find Lexie for our playdate in the snow.

I help Hal carry platters to the dining room for the other guests to enjoy when they wake while I wait for the girls.

He tells me where to find a set of sleds in the garage and loads a cardboard box with carrots and jelly beans for our snowman building.

Cobie and Lexie come barreling down the stairs, their excitement contagious as they pull on their boots, and we step out into the crisp winter morning.

We venture down the steps and across the yard, the deep snow crunching beneath our feet.

When we make it to the side of the inn, I ask, "All right, what do you guys want to do first?"

Laughter fills the air as they throw themselves backward into the fluffy snow, arms and legs moving in unison.

"Daddy, make snow angels with us," Cobie exclaims, her eyes sparkling.

I set the box aside and join them on the ground, and we flap our limbs side by side, creating imprints in the snow.

The wet snow clings to our clothes, but neither of them seems to mind.

I steal a glance at Cobie's face. Her smile is as bright as the early morning sun, and her eyes reflect pure joy.

In this moment, I realize how fleeting her childhood is and how important it is to cherish these simple times spent together.

I've missed so much.

We stand, and I help them brush the crystalized flakes from their coats.

"Look, Daddy, our snow angels are holding hands!" Cobie giggles as she points to our impressions.

"They sure are," I say and reach to my side, where my camera usually hangs.

It's not there.

I fight the urge to run back inside for it, choosing instead to commit the image to memory and be present with my girl.

"Who wants to help me build a snowman?" I ask.

"We do!" they shout in unison.

Lexie's mom and dad join us once they finish eating, and the five of us construct a snow family with carrot noses and jelly-bean eyes and smiles.

I snap branches from the brushes that line the front of the inn for arms, and Trixie offers the girls scarves and knit caps for their new icy friends.

We gather around our creations, and Trixie snaps a photo with her cell phone.

She and Lexie's mom leave us to prepare refreshments for the church, and her dad and I take our daughters sledding on the hill across the road.

It's by far the best day I've ever spent with my little girl.

After we warm up by the fire and eat lunch, Cobie showers and asks if she can go to the church with Bob and Trixie.

"I thought you and I were going to see the nativity together?"

"I've got a surprise," she tells me.

"What kind of surprise?" I ask as I help her into her jacket.

"I can't tell you. You'll have to wait and see!" she exclaims.

I pull the wool hat over her ears and kiss her forehead. "Okay, kid, I'll meet you there."

She waves as she takes Trixie's hand and trots off to Bob, who's waiting in the truck.

I ride with Dawn and Daniel, and the three of us park and make our way through the crowd that is milling around.

This time, my camera bag is secured on my shoulder.

We find the set, and it's like a scene straight out of a Bible story-book. Bran and Hannah, as Joseph and Mary, are standing together, their faces lit with adoration as they rock a swaddled baby in a hum-ble manger.

The gentle glow of the star mounted above them illuminates the makeshift stable. Shepherds with their staffs are gathered around a menagerie of live animals.

In the background to Joseph's left, I spot Cobie. She's wearing a white robe, and her curls are topped with a glittering golden ring.

She catches sight of us and breaks character.

"Daddy, I'm an angel!" she shouts as she waves.

"I see you, baby," I call as I unzip the leather bag at my hip.

I back up as I fit the entire scene into the shot.

I snap several photos, including close-ups of each actor and animal.

But as I click the last frame, something seems amiss.

The donkey by one of the shepherds brays loudly, startling the sheep nearby.

Hannah grabs hold of the squirming baby and struggles to stand as Bran rushes over and attempts to soothe the donkey, but only suc-ceeds in agitating the animal further.

Suddenly, chaos erupts.

The donkey, now completely spooked, bolts forward, knocking over one of the shepherds and trampling the manger.

The sheep, panicked by the sudden movement, scatter in all directions.

Hannah begins to shout at the goats, desperately trying to regain control of the situation, while Bran and the wise men try in vain to catch the escaping animals.

Daniel and I rush forward to help, and I manage to grab hold of the donkey's halter, bringing it to a stop just before it crashes into a trembling, wide-eyed Hannah, who backed up to shield Cobie and the other children from the stampede.

Bob and Hoyt attempt to corral the sheep, their experienced hands guiding them back toward the stable.

In the midst of the commotion, the audience, bundled up in winter coats and scarves, watches with a mix of amusement and concern.

Children giggle at the sight of the runaway animals while parents keep them at a safe distance.

Once the situation is under control, Bran and I share a chuckle, recognizing the humor in the situation as we work to calm the animals.

Hoyt walks to the front of the scene and addresses the crowd. "As we all know, live performances always come with an element of unpredictability. Thank you for your patience while we pull ourselves back together and get that hangry donkey some oats."

After a brief intermission and everything is back in its place, the nativity scene resumes, albeit with a new energy.

Dawn jots notes in her notebook.

"You aren't going to write about this, are you?" Hoyt asks as he joins us in the audience.

She grins as she reads from the page, *"The incident serves as a reminder of the beauty of imperfection and the resilience of community spirit. In the end, the live nativity scene might have gone awry, but it also became a memorable tale, a story that we could all laugh about because, sometimes, it's the unexpected moments that make the most cherished memories, reminding us of the true meaning of togetherness and the spirit of Christmas."*

She looks back up to Hoyt, who nods.

"I like that," he approves.

I catch sight of Sela and Linden, next to Hal's cocoa stand, and raise my camera to capture the moment as they sip from paper mugs and laugh, their breaths a visible mist in the cold air. Then, I feel the heat at my back.

"The camera loves her, doesn't it?"

I turn to see Norah grinning at me.

I glance down at the screen. "It does," I agree.

She moves past me, and walking backward, she calls, "Maybe you should ask her to take a horse and buggy ride with you. I bet you'd get some great photos of her and the lake from the carriage. You might even pass under some mistletoe along the route."

Hoyt leads Dawn and Daniel on a tour of the church, and I go in search of Sela.

I find her, Willa, and Norah standing in the carriage line.

"Oh, look who it is," Norah says as I approach.

"Hi, Isaac," Willa calls.

"Ladies," I greet.

Sela's eyes flicker to me, and her cheeks blush a sexy shade of pink.

"Do you want to ride with us?" Willa invites.

"I'd love to."

We make small talk as we await our turn.

"Hal said you're making dessert at the inn tonight," Willa says.

"I thought I'd make a Swedish Christmas dish and teach everyone a Scandinavian holiday tradition," I explain.

"How fun. The children are going to love that," she muses.

An intricately decorated white carriage pulls to a halt in front of us.

"Next," the driver calls as we step forward.

Norah grabs Willa's hand. "I forgot to get cocoa for the ride. You know I can't go without my cocoa."

Willa looks at her in confusion. "You can't?"

Norah widens her eyes and shakes her head, then turns to me.

"You and Sela take this one, and we'll catch another," she offers.

Willa finally catches on to her antics. "Right. You guys go ahead."

Sela looks at Willa's swollen belly and opens her mouth to protest, but Norah nudges her forward, and the driver takes hold of her hand to help her aboard.

She politely accepts his kindness, and I follow.

"There's a blanket if you two want it. The sun is setting, and it's going to be a chilly ride," he says before climbing into his seat and taking the reins.

The ornate wagon—pulled by two majestic chestnut-colored American saddlebreds, adorned with jingle bells—moves forward at his command onto the gravel path that encompasses the lake.

Moonlight dances on the water's surface, illuminating our path, as the wind whispers around us.

Sela snuggles into the warmth of my side as I spread the blanket across our laps and wrap my arm around her shoulders.

"Is that better?" I ask.

"Yes, thank you."

We ride in silence, admiring the view of the snow-covered trees standing tall in the distance as I hold her.

The air between us is thick with unspoken words.

I resist the urge to press my lips to her temple.

What are you doing, Isaac?

As if she can hear my internal thoughts, she turns into me and looks up. Her breath tickling the skin below my ear.

I glance at her face, her beautiful face, and she smiles.

I itch to pull out my camera to capture her expression. To steal it for myself.

My control melts with the heat in her gaze, and my free hand comes up and caresses her cheek as I lay a kiss on the tip of her nose.

Her eyes flutter shut as she sighs.

My lips travel to one corner of her mouth and then the other before landing on her lips.

This kiss is soft and full of unhurried longing. In this moment, the world around us fades, and so do all the reasons why I shouldn't kiss her.

Not the fact that we just met.

Not the fact that I'll be leaving tomorrow.

No, the only thing that matters is the intense connection between us.

Chapter Twelve

Sela

ISAAC HELPS ME DOWN FROM THE PADDED SEAT, AND I WALK AROUND to the front of the carriage to nuzzle the two magnificent stallions that led our romantic jaunt.

I open my purse and extract the small apples I brought for them.

The one on the right eagerly accepts the offered treat, its soft muzzle brushing against my palm.

"Thank you for the ride," I whisper as I run my hand down his side.

The other one neighs, and I laugh as I round to him.

"And thank you too," I say as I raise the other piece of red fruit to him.

I lean my forehead against his soft nose as he chews the treat.

Flashes of light in my peripheral vision draw my attention, and I see Isaac on one knee with his camera.

I give the animals one last caress and walk to him.

"You're supposed to be documenting the event, not wasting your time taking pictures of me," I scold.

"I can't help it. The camera loves you," he says as he stands.

We go in search of Cobie, and I tuck my hand into his elbow while he continues to capture the crowd with his lens.

He pauses at a table where ladies of the church are gifting nativity coloring books and a small package of crayons to the passing children.

He stops again at a booth where Hal is joyously greeting each visitor with a booming, "Merry Christmas," as he dishes out paper bags of kettle corn and Styrofoam cups of cocoa.

Dawn and Daniel find us after their ride around the lake with the mayor and his wife.

Daniel and Isaac get in line for refreshments as Dawn and I join Norah and Willa to warm our hands by a fire that Bob lit in a tin barrel near the booth.

"So, how does our little town measure up to the other holiday destinations you've covered?" I ask Dawn.

"To be honest, I didn't think places like this really existed. I'm a California girl, and I love the warm weather and beach life, but I could get used to spending time here as well."

"The lake has that effect on people," I say.

"Yeah, I think its charm is even rubbing off on our travel bug," she says.

"Who, Isaac?" I ask.

She nods.

I glance over at him as he photographs Hal.

"Lake Mistletoe is no Paris," I muse.

"And Paris is no Lake Mistletoe," Dawn adds.

Norah sighs. "How is that man single?"

Dawn laughs. "Right? If I wasn't married, I'd be all over him. I wanted to set him up with my best friend, Kelsey, but she's in culinary school, and between classes and her still licking her wounds over the last man, it never seemed to be a good time."

"Sela, you should totally take advantage of him," Norah urges.

"He's leaving tomorrow," I quip.

She taps my shoulder with hers. "I know that, but he's here now."

The boys return to us, their hands loaded down with bags of salty-sweet snacks.

"The nativity will be over soon. I need to head back to the inn to help Alice finish with dinner prep," Willa says.

"I'll find Mom, and we'll come with you," Norah says.

"You should come to eat with us, Sela," Willa invites.

Isaac's eyes come to me. "I know Cobie would love to spend one more evening with you before we go," he encourages.

"I'd love to."

The aroma of cinnamon and nutmeg fills the air as we stand around the island in the inn's kitchen.

With our bellies full of Alice's chili and cornbread, we all wait for Isaac to impart a lesson in Swedish Christmas porridge.

"Welcome to the heart of Swedish holiday traditions," he begins. "This porridge, or *julgröt*, is a cherished dish during Christmas in Sweden. It's a thick, sweet rice pudding that is served warm, but what makes it truly special is the hidden almond."

Cobie leans in, her eyes wide with curiosity. "Why do they hide the almond?" she asks.

Isaac smiles as he expertly measures the rice and milk. "During Christmas dinner, they serve the porridge from a large dish, and as they eat, the person who finds the almond in their bowl receives good luck for the year ahead. It's a bit like finding a treasure," he explains.

"But how do they make sure the almond stays hidden?" Cobie asks.

Isaac smiles. "That's the trick," he says. "Everyone in the family takes a turn stirring the porridge, making it nearly impossible to tell where the almond is."

One of the other children asks if they can stir the pot, and Isaac assists them as the porridge gently bubbles.

He patiently continues explaining the significance of the dish as they all line up for a turn to stir.

"In Sweden, Christmas isn't just about the presents or the feasts. It's about coming together, sharing moments, and embracing the spirit of togetherness. Finding the hidden almond is a symbol of good fortune and a reminder that life is full of surprises."

I love how a simple almond can bring so much joy.

Once the mixture thickens, Willa and I help ladle the creamy porridge into bowls.

Isaac tops each one with a sprinkle of cinnamon and a couple of raisins as Trixie passes each individual a spoon.

"Now, the best part. Let's see who of us is lucky enough to find the almond this time," Isaac says.

All the children climb onto stools while the adults stand around the island and dig into the delicious, warm porridge.

The room is filled with laughter and excited chatter, making the moment truly magical.

And as we reach the bottom of our bowls, Trixie squeals. There it is, the hidden almond, nestled among the grains in her dish, waiting to bring her all the luck.

The children gather around her legs and cheer as she scoops it up in her spoon and pops it into her mouth.

The crowd disperses when Hal announces there is gingerbread eggnog in the great room while we stay behind to clean the pot and load the dishwasher.

"That was amazing, Isaac. Thank you," Alice says.

"Yes, I think we might add porridge night to our traditions here at The Gingerbread Inn," Willa says.

Bob pops his head in the door. "Sela, Sammy is here to fetch us. Do you need a ride home?" he asks.

"Yes, I'll be just a moment. I'll meet them outside," I reply as I finish rinsing the bowl in my hand and adding it to the machine's rack.

Alice and Willa go to say their good-byes to Norah and Trixie, leaving Isaac and me alone.

I guess this is it.

A heavy feeling settles in my chest as the thought that I might never see him or Cobie again sinks in.

I open my mouth to speak, but he quiets me when he steps in and takes my mouth with his.

"I don't want to say good-bye yet," he whispers against my lips.

"Me neither," I murmur.

"I'm going by Hannah's shop to see Bran's boat after I put Cobie to bed. Can I come see you after?" he asks.

"I'll leave the shop door open for you. Just lock it when you get there. The stairs to my loft are behind the glass flower case."

He gives me one more quick kiss, and then I step out of the kitchen in search of Cobie.

I find her and Lexie sitting at the coffee table in front of the stone fireplace, writing a wish on a slip of paper and stuffing it into their wishing bottle.

"Hi, Cobie. I just wanted to say good-bye. I hope you and your daddy have a wonderful Christmas in Paris," I say as I bend down to her.

She hesitates for a moment before standing and throwing her arms around me in a tight hug.

"I'll miss you, Sela," she cries.

I wrap my arms around her and pull her close.

"I'll miss you too, sweet girl. I had the most fun with you these past few days. Oh, I have something for you."

I stand and find the package where I hid it under the Christmas tree. I pick it up and hand it to her.

"Can I open it?"

I nod.

She sits on the sofa and carefully tugs the bow and paper from the box. Once it's open, she peels back the layer of tissue to reveal the gift inside.

"What is it?" she asks.

"It's a carved map of the state of Idaho. I placed a star right over Lake Mistletoe. That way, you can always find your way back," I explain as I point to the tiny gold star nestled in the raised mountains.

She sniffles as she clutches the map to her chest.

"Will I see you again?" she asks.

I lean back and give her a bright smile. "I'll give your dad my phone number, and you can video-chat me anytime you want. Deal?"

She grins. "Deal."

Chapter Thirteen

Isaac

I TAKE A SOMBER LITTLE GIRL UP TO BED.

"What time do we have to leave?" she asks as I tuck the covers around her tightly.

"Our plane leaves from the Boise Airport at five in the evening. We need to be there two hours before that, and it takes two and a half hours to drive to the airport from here," I explain.

She furrows her brows as she makes the calculation. "So, if we leave at noon, we'll be on time."

I tap the tip of her nose. "Good job, but we have to return the SUV to the rental company too, remember? I think we should say eleven to be on the safe side," I tell her.

"Eleven. That means we can have breakfast with Alice and Trixie and Willa and Lexie before we leave!" She opens her hand and counts off her new friends on her fingers.

"Yes. If you promise to go right to sleep so we can get up early in the morning and pack."

She rolls to her side instantly and closes her eyes.

I chuckle. "I'm going out for a bit. If you need anything, Willa and Keller are right downstairs."

She opens one eye. "Okay, Daddy. Good night."

I bend and brush her hair from her face and kiss her forehead. "Sweet dreams, baby."

I quietly grab the keys to the SUV, my coat, and my camera bag before turning off the lamp and closing the door.

Willa meets me at the bottom of the steps.

"Thank you for keeping an ear out for Cobie," I say.

"It's not a problem. Annette has the night off, so Keller and I plan to hunker down in the great room so we can check in any late arrivals. Take your time. I'll peek in on her in a bit."

"You have my number if you need me?"

She smiles. "Yep. It's in our system. So, go on and get out of here."

She shoos me out of the door.

When I make it to the SUV, I glance at the time.

I text Bran to get the address, and once he replies, I throw the SUV in reverse and race to meet him.

I pull into the back of Smitten in the Lake Mistletoe Event Services building to find the roll-up garage door open to the chilly night.

Bran and his father are standing over a metal frame, wearing face shields, sparks dancing around them like fireflies as they operate the welding torch.

I manage to snap a few frames before they notice my presence.

"Hey, Isaac," Bran greets as he lifts the mask and tugs off his gloves. "This is my dad."

I walk inside and shake the older version of Bran's hand.

"It's nice to meet you, Mr. Prince," I greet.

"Please call me Norris," he says.

I nod. "Norris."

Bran leads me deeper inside the building so I can check out their boat design.

"That's brilliant," I say as I look over the drawings.

"How do you think it'll do against Bob's design?" Bran asks.

I slide my eyes to him and grin. "Oh, no, I'm not giving up any secrets. I'm Switzerland in this competition," I say.

He laughs.

"Do you mind if I get a few more pics for the magazine?"

"No, go right ahead." He gives his permission.

I stay and watch them work. The skill they put into every piece of the model is impressive.

"You'll have to send me a photo of the completed boat," I request as Bran walks me out to the SUV.

"I'll do that. It was nice meeting you and your daughter. You and Cobie have a safe trip."

"Thanks, and merry Christmas."

He and Norris stand in the doorway and wave until I make the turn toward downtown and lose sight of them.

I park in a lot a couple of blocks from the flower shop and step out onto the sidewalk. My footsteps echo down the deserted downtown streets as I walk. The shops that are usually bustling with life are silent and shrouded in darkness, their windows reflecting the falling snowflakes like stars in the night sky.

I pull my coat tighter around me, the chill of the winter night seeping through the fabric and into my bones.

When I make it to the door, I tug it gently to find it is still unlocked.

A bell chimes, and I fish my phone from my pocket and click the flashlight on so I can see to twist the dead bolt behind me.

I locate the staircase hidden behind the glass display case and take the steps two at a time until I reach a scarred wooden door.

I try the doorknob before knocking and find she's left it unlocked for me as well.

I step inside the tiny studio apartment. There is a wide sectional sofa and ottoman to the left, and a small, round dining table with three mismatched chairs in front of a sleek kitchenette.

The glow from the white lights of the petite Christmas tree illuminates a silhouette curled in a ball on the queen-size bed that is propped against the far wall.

I tug off my coat and boots and set them by the door before going to her.

Taking a seat on the edge of the bed, I commit the sight of her sleeping to memory.

Her long, dark lashes are resting against her pink cheeks. Light-brown hair is twisted into a messy knot, held in place on top of her head by a silk hair tie. Her mouth is parted and releases a light snore with every breath.

I have to resist the overwhelming urge to pull her into my lap and strip the oversize T-shirt she's wearing from her body as I kiss the sleep from her eyes.

The jostle of my weight dipping the mattress causes her to rouse, and she blinks up at me.

"Isaac?"

Her voice is raspy from sleep, and I swear my body reacts to the sexy sound.

"I'm sorry I'm so late," I whisper.

She rises to her elbows. "What time is it?" she asks.

"Just past eleven."

She raises her arms above her, and a yawn escapes as she extends her back in a deep stretch, causing the hem of her shirt to rise, exposing the top of her thighs.

She's trying to kill me.

Sitting up, she scooches to the left side of the bed and pats the space beside her in invitation. "Want to watch a movie with me?" she asks.

I shouldn't.

I should tell her I have to go.

I should tell her it was lovely to meet her.

I should kiss her on the cheek and tell her good-bye.

I should walk my ass back downstairs and get in the SUV and leave.

I should do all of those things, but instead, I throw my legs on the bed and scoot over to join her.

"What are we watching?" I ask.

She plucks the remote from the nightstand and clicks the television that's mounted on the wall to life.

"*Elf* or *Christmas Vacation*. The choice is yours," she replies.

I stuff one of her pillows behind me and cross my arms over my chest as I settle back against the headboard.

"I think I hear a *funny squeaky sound*," I say.

She cuts her eyes to me and grins. "Got it!"

She finds *National Lampoon's Christmas Vacation* on her list and hits pause before going to her knees and crawling down the bed.

I reach out and grab hold of her foot. She comes to a stop and looks over her shoulder at me.

"Where are you going?" I ask.

"To make popcorn and open a bottle of wine, duh. You can't have a movie night without snacks."

I release her, and she slips off the edge and shuffles to the wine rack that sits on the counter between the stove and the wall. She takes her time choosing a bottle of red and patters over to me with an opener. I take them from her hand, and she returns to toss a bag of popcorn into the microwave. While it pops, she pulls two glasses from the cabinet and returns to wait for me to twist the cork from the bottle. I slip the cork into my pocket before filling the glasses. She sets them on the nightstand and takes the bottle back to the counter.

When she returns, she is carrying a large bowl filled with salty, popped kernels. I take it as she climbs over me, and we bed down to watch the movie.

Chapter Fourteen

Sela

THE COZY WARMTH OF THE MAN LYING NEXT TO ME, SHARING A bowl of buttery popcorn, envelops me.

On the television screen, the classic holiday movie plays, and we both laugh at the antics of Clark Griswold. Our eyes are glued to the screen when Isaac reaches for another handful of popcorn, his fingers brushing against mine. A jolt of electricity shoots through me at the contact, making my heart skip a beat.

He turns his head to look at me, his eyes sparkling with mischief and something more. "Sela."

The raspy way my name rolls off his tongue causes my breath to catch in my throat.

I steal a glance at his lips, my mind racing with emotions at the thought that this will probably be the last time he says my name.

Before I can overthink it, I lean in, closing the distance between us.

Our lips meet in a soft, sweet kiss, sending fireworks exploding in my belly.

Time seems to stand still as I savor the moment.

Hannah's words rattle around in my mind. *"Nothing wrong with a little Christmas fling."*

A Christmas fling. Why not?

My nether regions agree, and I press my body closer to his.

I groan in protest when his mouth leaves mine, but he quickly sets the bowl aside. Then, his hand fists into my tee, and he pulls me forward. His mouth is on mine, and he tastes of wine. Suddenly, all hesitation flies from my brain, and the only thing I want is to feel him.

I bring my leg over his hip and slide on top of him.

His hands grip the hem of my shirt and pull it up. I sit up and raise my arms to help, and he tosses it to the floor. I'm sitting before him in a black lace bra and panties.

His eyes caress my skin as he takes me in.

He takes one strap between his fingers and slides it off my shoulder. The strap drops to my elbow, exposing one breast.

He glides his other hand up my rib cage and cups the curve while running the rough pad of his thumb over my nipple. A tremor runs through me, and the bud tightens into a taut pebble. The sensation causes me to gasp as he releases me, reaches behind my back, and flicks the fasteners holding the bra in place. It falls from my body and into his lap between us.

He swallows hard as he looks at me.

My eyes meet his, and I can see the need burning there.

The same need that is pulsing through my veins.

He must see it, too, because he lowers his head and sucks one of my nipples into his warm mouth.

My hands thread into the hair at the nape of his neck, and I hold him to me as he nips and licks then pulls back and switches to the other breast. My hips rise as he runs his teeth across it, and my hands fall from his head to his sides, beginning to yank at his shirt.

"It's not fair that I'm sitting here, naked, and you still have all your clothes on," I whisper.

He disengages and sits back to let me remove his shirt, and I rake my nails down the front of his chest and into the scattering of dark hair above his abs. I tug gently, and he groans.

My hand ventures lower until it finds the snap on his jeans.

I flick it open, and my eyes meet his as my hand finds him.

His cock jerks at the contact as I wrap my fingers around him.

"Fuuuck."

His eyes close as I squeeze.

"Sela," he grunts.

He reaches around and grabs my hips and pulls me forward. Then, he bears up and flips me to my back, coming on top of me.

He goes to his knees, and then he lifts one of my ankles and kisses his way up the inside of my thigh. When he reaches the apex, he places a kiss on my center and hooks his fingers in the lace, tugging my panties off before bringing my leg up and over his shoulder.

I hold my breath as I watch, letting my other leg fall to the side, welcoming him.

He takes two fingers and parts my lips, opening me to him, and he drags his tongue through the wetness.

My hips flex at the contact as he sucks my clit deep.

I moan, and one hand finds his hair. I hold him where I need him as he devours me. His tongue finds my opening, and I start thrusting against it.

He gives me what my body wants, and I ride his tongue until I am a panting and whimpering mess. Then, he brings his mouth back to my bud and slides a finger inside me. He twists and curls until he finds just the right spot that makes me cry out in agonizing pleasure.

He adds another finger and nips at my clit until my legs begin to quiver and I clamp my thighs to his ears. He continues to lick as I get lost in the sensation that carries me away.

Once my breathing slows and my grip on him eases, he stands and fishes a foil packet from his pocket. He takes it between his teeth before sliding his jeans and underwear down and kicking them to the side. He tears the packet open, and I watch as he guides the latex over himself before returning to me.

I snake my arms around his neck and lace my fingers through his hair.

He hesitates for a moment, and then he bends down and presses his lips to mine. I open to him immediately, and he deepens the kiss. He nips at my bottom lip and then soothes it with his tongue. His weight shifts fully on top of me, and I wrap my legs around his hips as he settles between them.

I am completely exposed to him.

There is nothing between us, and I can feel every hard inch of him. He threads his fingers through the hair at the side of my face and kisses me hard as he moves to my entrance and pauses.

My nails score down his bare back in response.

I grab his ass and lunge up to bring him into me. His tip enters, and I moan as he slowly rocks forward until he is seated completely inside me.

Filling me.

His hips begin to slowly move, driving him further inside of me, and it feels so good. I lock my legs around his waist, and I thrust up to meet him, taking him deeper and deeper until I'm screaming his name into the dark room as I climax.

"Isaac!"

He quickens his pace until he lets out a cry of his own. I wrap my arms around him and hold on until he finishes and collapses on top of me.

We lie there, a sweaty, entangled mess, while we catch our breath, and then he falls onto his back.

I roll over onto my side, and contentment rushes over me as I snuggle into him.

Contentment, followed quickly by sadness.

This was a good-bye.

I wake up to sunlight piercing through the window above the sink.

My body aches from last night's activities. I stretch as my eyes blink open, and I reach to my right.

The bed is empty beside me.

When I sit up and look around the room, my eyes catch on the slip of paper sitting on the nightstand with one of the flower shop's pens atop it.

I grab it and read the scribbled message.

Sela,

I needed to get back to the inn before Cobie missed me. You looked so peaceful, and even though I wanted to say good-bye, it would be too hard to leave if you were awake. Thank you for showing me around Lake Mistletoe this week and for being so kind to my little girl. We will both miss you.

—Isaac

I clasp the note to my chest as I hold back the tears that have gathered at the corners of my eyes.

You knew he was leaving.

I scold myself for being so emotional. Then, I pull it together and get up to get dressed and meet Norah.

After a hot shower, I pull on a pair of leggings and a cowl-necked sweater and tug on my comfy fur-lined boots. I braid my hair to the side and forgo makeup.

I make it downstairs, and Norah is already tooling around the shop with a watering can in hand.

When she hears my footsteps, she turns to me.

"Good morning, sunshine," she starts. "Whoa, what's wrong?" she asks as she takes me in.

"Isaac spent the night," I confess.

"I would have expected a little more afterglow from the experience," she says.

I sniffle. "He's gone."

She drops the vessel and opens her arms.

I run to her, and she wraps her arms around me.

"I forgot it was today," she murmurs.

I nod into her chest.

"I think it's time to drown your sorrows."

"Absolutely," I sob.

"What shall it be—wine, cookies, eggnog? Tequila shots?" she asks.

"Yes," I mumble.

"I'll call the girls," she says as she pats my back.

Chapter Fifteen

Isaac

M Y HEART RACES AS PANIC TIGHTENS ITS GRIP. I'VE SCOURED our room, tearing through our suitcases and rifling through drawers in a desperate search for the missing bag. The small navy bag that holds my and Cobie's passports and airline tickets—the gateway to our long-awaited Christmas holiday in Paris.

"Where can it be?" I mutter, my voice quivering with worry.

Cobie is on her knees by the credenza, her eyes scanning the floor. "I don't see it, Daddy," she calls.

I vividly recall placing the passports in the bag when we landed in Boise after checking the flight details one last time. Then, I tucked the bag into the front zippered compartment of my suitcase.

Didn't I?

I know I double-checked that I had everything before we disembarked from the airplane, and I think it was with our things when I loaded them into the rental, but now, it's like the bag has vanished into thin air.

"I'm going to go check the backseat of the SUV. You keep looking," I tell her.

She nods, and I run down the stairs.

I have to find those passports. The joy of spending quality time with Cobie hangs in the balance, threatened by the absence of the crucial documents.

Keller is standing in the foyer. "Still can't find it?" he asks.

"Nope. I'm going to check the SUV," I say as I hurry past him.

"I'll have Annette talk to the staff and see if any of them saw the bag," he offers.

"Thanks."

I search the SUV, front and back and even the trunk.

"Shit!" I scream as I slam the passenger door shut.

I glance down at my watch and see it's a quarter till noon.

We're cutting it too close.

I stomp back to the front door, and Annette has joined Keller at reception.

"I'm sorry, Isaac, but no one recalls seeing a blue crossbody," she informs me.

"Have you called the airport to see if anyone turned it in there?" Keller asks.

I shake my head. "No, that's a good idea though," I note.

"I'll look up the number and call for you," she offers as she pecks at her keyboard before picking up the inn's landline.

Keller clasps my shoulder. "We'll find it."

"I just hope it's not too late," I say.

"Maybe the airline can book you guys on a later flight," he suggests.

"Maybe," I agree.

Annette speaks to someone over the phone. When she clicks off, she turns to us.

"No luck. They checked the lost and found. I left your name and number with them in case it shows up," she says.

"It's not likely after a week," I mutter.

Cobie hurries down the stairs, her pink suitcase thumping on every step along the way as she tugs it behind her.

"Daddy, did you find it?" she asks.

"No, baby, not yet."

Her eyes fill with tears. "But we have to go now. It's past eleven," she cries.

I scoop her up into my arms and hug her close. "Don't worry. I'll fix this."

She sobs into my chest as I wonder just how I'm going to do that.

"I need a copy of her birth certificate. Can you overnight it to me?" I ask Lonnie.

"What good is that going to do?" she asks.

"There's a passport agency in Boise. If I have both our birth certificates and new photos made, they can hopefully process them the same day and get us new books," I explain.

"Do you have yours?" she asks.

"I called my mother first. She's looking to see if she has a copy," I reply.

She sighs. "Where do you want it sent?"

I give her the address to the inn.

"It's too late to get it out today," she says.

"I know."

"And your mother will probably not be able to find a copy of yours," she continues.

"I know that too."

"I'll see if there's a copy here somewhere. I used to have it in the safe with mine and Cobie's, but I don't know if I still have it."

"Thank you."

"I can't promise I do," she quips.

"I appreciate you looking all the same."

The line goes silent, and I know she wants to say more.

"Spit it out, Lonnie."

"It's not that big of a deal, Isaac, if you don't make it to Paris. You did insure the trip, right?"

"I did, but I don't want to disappoint Cobie and ruin her Christmas," I bark.

"Oh, for goodness' sake, Isaac. She's eight years old. The only thing that can ruin her Christmas is you," she snaps.

"Me?"

"Yes, you. Do you know what she talks about every time she video-calls me?" she asks.

"What?"

"The things you guys are doing in Lake Mistletoe. *Daddy took me to get cocoa. Daddy helped me decorate cookies. Daddy and I made snow angels and built a snowman. Daddy and I found an elf.* She doesn't need a fancy trip or expensive gifts, Isaac. The only thing that matters to that little girl is watching holiday movies, eating all the Christmas cookies, trying her best to stay up in hopes of catching a glimpse of Santa and his reindeer, and being with you. Wherever that is," she spells out.

"I just wanted to make it a Christmas she'd never forget," I mutter.

"So, get to doing that," she commands.

"When did you get so wise?" I ask.

"I've always been wise. You were just too unwise to realize it," she clarifies.

I chuckle. "Thanks, Lonnie."

"You're welcome. I'll let you know if and when I find what you need."

I end the call and dial the customer service number for the airline and explain the situation.

They credit my account for the tickets we are unable to use so that I can use the funds to book us on a later flight. Then, I contact the owner of the Airbnb I booked in Paris and let him know that we won't be arriving this evening.

Cobie climbs into my lap. "Are you angry or sad?" she asks.

I smile down at her. "I'm just frustrated with myself for losing our passports and causing us to miss our flights," I admit.

She takes my chin into her little hands. "It's okay, Daddy. Don't be frustrated."

I place my forehead against hers. "I'll try."

"We should take a nap. Mommy says naps help me when I'm irritable," she declares.

I laugh as I stand with her in my arms. "I think a nap sounds like a wonderful idea."

Chapter Sixteen

Sela

Norah, Hannah, Willa, and I are sitting in Norah's living room, stuffing our faces with cookies and spiked eggnog. Except for Willa. She is partaking in virgin nog as a show of solidarity with my misery.

"So, you and Isaac … you know?" Willa asks.

Norah cuts her eyes to Willa. "What are we, kindergartners?" she asks.

Willa rolls her eyes.

"Yeah, we … you know," I reply.

"How was it?" Hannah asks.

"Fun. Toe-curling. Amazing," I answer.

"Just what the doctor ordered. I bet your nether regions are happy," Norah sings.

"Giddy," I confirm.

"It's too bad you waited until his last night," Hannah says.

My head swings to her. "As opposed to the first night we met? He's only been here a week," I say.

"Right," she quips.

"Oh God, I'm such a slut," I cry as I drop my head into my hands.

The three of them start to giggle.

"It's not funny," I murmur.

Norah shoves my shoulder. "Stop slut-shaming yourself. You're a grown woman who had a toe-curling night with a sexy visitor. You're allowed."

I peek up at them. "I guess I'm not used to having one-night stands," I admit.

"You like him," Willa guesses.

"I do. Not that it matters."

"You never know. Things always have a way of working themselves out," Hannah says.

Sammy arrives with our lunch.

"They didn't have cookies and cream, so I got chocolate and cherry vanilla," he says as Norah pulls the tubs of ice cream from the bag.

"That will have to do," she says.

He kisses her cheek. "Knock yourselves out."

Willa stands and walks to the counter, looking at her phone.

"I'm going to have to pass. Keller texted. It seems Isaac and Cobie lost their passports and missed their flight. Everyone is searching the inn, looking for them."

"What? They're still here?" I sputter.

Her eyes come to mine, and she grins. "Yep. Looks like they're stranded."

The three of us pile into Sammy's truck and head to the inn.

My stomach fills with butterflies the closer we get.

"Maybe I should go home," I say.

Norah looks over her shoulder into the backseat and glares at me. "Why would you do that?"

"Because I'm feeling a little woozy," I say.

"It's the eggnog. I told you that you were being heavy-handed with the brandy," Hannah tells Norah.

"We were drinking her sorrows away. I did what I had to do," Norah huffs.

Willa takes my hand and holds it tightly. "Just breathe," she coaches.

I do as she said and take several calming breaths.

I'm being ridiculous. So we had a passionate night together. We are two single, consenting adults.

"You look like you're going to hurl. Pull it together, girl. You have no reason to feel awkward," Norah encourages.

"I know. I just didn't expect to see him again."

"It's the lake working its magic again," Hannah assesses.

I laugh. "It's a hiccup in Isaac's plans. I'm sure he'll find their passports, and they'll be on the next flight to France."

Norah points at me. "You have no faith in the lake. We know different."

Willa looks at me and shrugs. "She's right. It works in mysterious ways. Even if he does leave in a day or so, you have now. Enjoy it."

She's right. Even if it's only another twenty-four hours, I look forward to more time with Isaac and Cobie.

A gift. Thanks, Santa.

Sammy parks at the inn, and as we step out onto the driveway, a whirl of bouncing curls comes flying in our direction.

"Whoa," I bellow as Cobie barrels into me and wraps her arms around my legs.

"We didn't leave, Sela," she cries.

I look down at her. "I can see that."

She lets me go and takes a step back. "Daddy's upset," she says.

"What about you?" I ask.

She shrugs. "I'm sad for him, but I like it here."

Norah steps beside her and tousles her hair. "Well, we're happy you're still around, kiddo. You've been a big help, and we still have a ton of stuff to do before the Christmas Market next weekend. Are you up to the task?" Norah asks, raising an eyebrow at Cobie.

"Yes, ma'am. I'm ready!"

She follows Norah to the front door just as Isaac emerges. He moves aside so they can enter the inn, and then he looks skyward, squeezes his eyes shut, and blows out a long, frustrated breath. A hand tugging at his rumpled hair.

He looks weary.

I take a couple of timid steps forward when his eyes open and his gaze turns in my direction.

"Hi," I say.

He doesn't return the greeting. Instead, he darts down the stairs, picks me up off my feet, and crushes me against him in a hug. My hands go to his neck, and I hold him tightly.

"I'm sorry your plans got messed up," I whisper.

He groans. "I'm so mad at myself," he mumbles.

"You didn't lose them on purpose," I assure him.

He releases me and drops me to my feet.

"Yeah, don't be so hard on yourself."

I look over my shoulder, where Willa and Hannah have come up behind us.

"I know, but now, I have no idea what we're going to do. I have no backup plan for the holidays, and I'm sure you guys are all booked for the rest of the year."

Willa winces.

"I thought so," he says.

"We'll figure something out; don't worry," she assures him.

Trixie's head pops out of the door. "Anyone hungry?" she asks.

"Yes!" Willa, Hannah, and I call at once.

"Great, I made turkey potpies for lunch. Come and get it while it's hot," she commands.

Willa and Hannah hurry past us and into the inn. I take Isaac's hand and thread my fingers with his.

"There's nothing that can't be solved over a slice of Trixie's potpie," I say.

He grins. "Is that right?"

"A bona fide fact," I say.

The butterflies in my stomach dissipate as he lets me lead him inside.

Chapter Seventeen

Isaac

"TRIXIE, THIS IS AMAZING. YOU SHOULD BE SELLING THESE IN supermarkets," I praise as I take another bite of the flaky pie.

"Thank you, Isaac. I made them with herb-infused gravy this time. I think it gives it a little extra something," she replies.

"It's like Thanksgiving in a pie," I agree.

Keller joins us at the table, and Alice sets a plate in front of him.

"Thank you," he says.

Alice pats his cheek as Trixie passes him the platter of individual pastries.

"Any luck, Isaac?" he asks as he spoons an extra helping of gravy on top.

"No. I must have dropped it at the airport or at the car rental agency when I was grabbing my identification. It's the only explanation."

"You should just stay here. Daniel and I will be in town until the Holly Ball. It'll be nice to get photos of the rest of the festivities," Dawn suggests.

I give her a tight smile.

"Yes, you guys should stay," Trixie agrees.

Cobie's pleading eyes come to me from her place across the table, next to Lexie. "Can we, Daddy?" she asks.

"Annette checked, and our room isn't available after tonight," I tell her.

Her face falls.

"You can stay with me and Bran," Hannah offers.

"No, we discussed it already. Alice and Hal can stay with me and Bob at our house, and you two can move to their room here," Trixie declares.

My eyes flit to a smiling Alice. "I can't ask you to do that," I say.

"You didn't," she quips.

"But you start your day so early already," I begin.

Her hand shoots into the air to stop me. "We insist. Trixie's house is only minutes away, and Dawn's right; it'll be nice to have photos of the boat parade, Christmas Market, and Holly Ball. Plus, Cobie and Lexie promised to pitch in at the Inn Hop." She glances at my daughter and winks.

These people are something else. We've only known them for a few short days, and they feel like family. I'm beginning to understand why guests return to the inn year after year. They claim you.

"Daddy?"

Cobie's voice pulls me from my thoughts.

"Okay. We'll stay until our passports are found."

"Yay," Lexie howls as she throws her arms around Cobie.

My gaze slides to Sela, who is quietly enjoying her meal.

Her lips turn up in a slight smile as she chews.

Bran's truck pulls in as Keller and I are carrying more wood inside.

"Hey, I heard you are staying in town," he says as he grabs an armful and follows.

"Looks like it," I reply.

"So, that means you can help with our parade entry now," he states.

Keller looks over his shoulder. "No way. He's our guest. If anyone can claim him, it's me."

Bran scowls at him. "You and Bob already have Barry and Sammy if you need them," he gripes.

"So?"

"So, don't be stingy. Or are you just scared?" Bran teases.

Keller drops the logs beside the fireplace and turns to face us. "He's seen our plans."

Bran nods. "I know. And I've already tried prying details out of him. He's a vault," Bran informs him.

Keller crosses his arms over his chest. "Fine. You can have Isaac, but that's it. One of him equals both of my brothers-in-law."

"Fair enough," Bran agrees.

They both look at me.

"I'm in."

Bran slaps me on the back. "Glad to hear it. Dad and I will be back at it tonight. I'll supply the beer."

"Is it okay if I bring Cobie along?" I ask.

"Sure. A woman's perspective is always welcome. Besides, Mom, Hannah, and Sela will be there too. They're working on some of Willa's baby shower favors at Hannah's office," he says.

We carry in the rest of the wood, and some of the tension in my chest eases as I catch sight of Cobie and Lexie ambushing a few of the older boys with snowballs in the front yard.

Cobie giggles with glee as she and her new friend take off running for cover as the boys gather snow to retaliate. They return fire but are gentle in their assault on the little girls, letting them reach the safety of cover before they start tossing the packed missiles in their direction.

Bob's truck turns into the drive, and he taps his horn to get our attention.

"What's up, Pop?" Keller asks as Bob rolls down the driver's window.

"Your mom and Alice have decided they want to make a fresh trout dinner tomorrow," he replies.

Keller turns to Bran. "What do you think? Can we close up shop at noon?" he asks.

"I say we take the entire day off," Bran suggests.

"You close your store for a trout dinner?" I question.

Keller grins. "Trout dinner means we get to go ice fishing," he explains.

"Ice fishing?" I repeat.

"Yep. It's tradition. We'll take some of the boys and their fathers or grandfathers up the mountain to ice fish at Magic Reservoir. You wanna come?" Bob asks.

"Yeah, the kids love it. We try to take them at least once every year," Keller adds.

"I've never been ice fishing before," I admit.

"It's like regular fishing. Just colder, and you need an auger," Bran explains.

"The auger's already loaded on the back of the truck," Bob says.

"What happens if we don't catch any fish?" I ask.

"Then, we stop at the fish market on the way back. The ladies won't know the difference," Bob says.

"I'm in," I respond.

"Great. I'll throw an extra rod and reel in the pickup for you. We leave after breakfast."

Bob offers his good-bye and reverses out of the driveway.

"They totally know the difference," Bran mutters.

"Yep," Keller agrees as he waves to his father.

"What size boots do you wear?" Bran asks me as he looks down at my sneaker-covered feet.

"Ten and a half. Why? I have boots," I say.

"Yeah, but you'll need a pair of waterproof waders. Lake water and slush will cover your feet when we drill into the ice. I have a pair that should fit you," he says.

"And I have an extra rain bib you can wear," Keller adds.

"Anything else I need?" I ask.

"Double layer of wool socks, waterproof gloves, and sunglasses," Bran advises.

Those I have.

Chapter Eighteen

Isaac

"**W**E'RE GOING TO BUILD A BOAT?"

I glance over at Cobie, who is buckled into the passenger seat of the SUV.

"Technically, we're decorating the boat for a Christmas parade on the lake, but Bran and his dad are taking two kayaks and creating a boat, so, yeah, I guess we are building a boat," I explain.

"You don't build stuff," she points out.

I nod. "That's true, but Bran does, and I can follow directions, so he and his dad are going to teach me."

"Will you get a prize, too, if they win?"

I smile at my inquisitive girl. "I think it's a single blue ribbon and bragging rights."

She nods. "At least we can say our team won."

"Exactly," I agree.

I pull around to the back of the building and park next to Bran's truck. The garage doors are open once again, and Sela is leaning over Bran's shoulders, watching him as he secures a bracket to one of the kayaks.

Cobie unbuckles and grabs her door handle.

Before I have time to make it around the hood of the truck to help her, she has jumped down.

"Sela!" she yells as she sprints down the asphalt toward them.

Sela looks up and smiles wide as she bends to catch my little girl in her open arms.

She squeezes her for a moment before she releases her and stands.

"I didn't know you were going to be here," Cobie says.

"Yep. Mom and I are going to help Hannah put together guest gifts for Willa's baby shower. Do you want to help?"

"What do you want me to do?" Cobie asks.

"Mom brought honey she and Dad harvested from their bees a couple of months ago, and we're going to fill miniature jars. I printed blue labels for them that say, *A little honey is on the way*. Then, we are going to put them in a green organza bag with a honey dipstick and tie it with a yellow bow. You can fill the bags and tie the bows. Hannah's making homemade goat milk soaps and pouring it into safari animal molds. When they cool, we'll help her put those in bags with a tag that says, *From our baby to yours*."

"Soap and honey?" Bran asks.

Sela shrugs. "Not everyone likes honey. Hannah wants the guest to have options."

"Who doesn't like honey?" Norris bellows.

Cobie turns to me. "Daddy, I know I said I'd help with the boat, but Sela needs me."

"I indeed do," Sela agrees.

I flit my eyes between the two of them.

"All right. You can assist the ladies. But Sela is in charge. You have to mind her."

Cobie reaches up and takes Sela's hand. "Okay."

Sela leads her into the office, and I join the fellas.

"That little one of yours is adorable," Norris says as I settle into a folding chair beside him.

"That she is," I agree.

"She doesn't seem too upset about your trip being delayed," he assesses.

"No, she's resilient. Besides, she likes it here."

He nods. "I imagine most kids would. It's a magical place," he muses.

It certainly is.

Bran takes a seat in front of us. "I've been doing some thinking, and I have an idea that could clinch the ribbon for us," he says.

Norris raises an eyebrow as we both listen to what he has in mind.

"Son, I know about the judges, but the crowd will sure be excited," Norris tells him.

"I think so too. It'll be the largest blown globe I've ever done. But it will be an eye-catcher."

The design is simple. We are joining two green kayaks together with a metal frame. The frame will encase a rotating wooden platform that will serve as the base for a life-sized snow globe. Hanging from the top of the thin glass globe will be a large, lit mistletoe. Bran and Hannah will be posing on the platform, giving one another a Christmas kiss, as machines hidden under their feet blow fake snow in the globe around them with a surprise for the spectators.

"It's brilliant," I agree.

Bran smiles as he stands. "Let's get to it. We have a week to finish it all."

"How are you going to get the glass done without Keller seeing it?" I ask.

"He's already seen it. I told him I was commissioned by Sun Valley to make a life-sized snow globe for the resort. He didn't question it."

"Sneaky," Norris quips.

"All fair in love and boat wars," Bran mutters.

The two of them fire up the welding torches, and I get to work on painting the kayaks a deep wintergreen.

We work for several hours, and then Linden comes in, bearing snacks. Bran grabs us all a beer from the small fridge in the corner of the garage, and we take a break.

"The frame is done, and the kayaks are painted. We'll let them dry overnight, and I'll hand-paint a snowy mountain scene with tall evergreens on the sides tomorrow once we get back from fishing. Then, Tuesday, we can come back after dinner and attach the frame and the turntable for the platform. We can weld a track to the edges to hold the globe. I'll need some help loading and getting the glass work over here. It's not super heavy, but it's fragile, and we'll need all hands on deck to set it," Bran explains.

"How are you and Hannah getting in and out of the thing?" I ask.

"I'm cutting a door in one side, and we can affix a split plastic curtain over it. That way, it's still transparent but will hold in the snowflakes."

"We should get a couple of speakers and blast an instrumental version of 'I Saw Mommy Kissing Santa Claus' as you two spin," I suggest.

Bran raises a brow. "I like that idea. A mic would come in handy too," he says.

"I'll run by the hardware store and see what I can find," I offer.

Bran clasps my shoulder. "It sucks that you got stranded and weren't able to go on your trip, but I'm sure glad you're here, buddy. This boat is going to be epic."

We finish our pigs in a blanket and chips and get back to work.

I carry a sleeping Cobie to the SUV.

She fell asleep on the sofa in Hannah's office about thirty minutes ago.

Once I have her strapped into the backseat, I help Sela load the cardboard boxes, filled with their colorful party favors, into the trunk.

"Thanks for taking these to the inn for us," she says as I shut the liftgate.

"It's no trouble at all," I say.

"Keller knows you're coming, and he'll help you carry them into the atrium. You can set them on the table by the stage."

"Got it," I say.

"Okay, well, I'll let you go. Thank you again."

I catch her hand as she spins to go.

"Wait, Sela."

She turns back to me, and her big, beautiful eyes come to me.

I know I need to say something after the night we spent together, but I can't find the right words.

"How are you getting home?" I ask instead.

"Mom and Dad are going to drop me off," she says.

"I can give you a ride. I mean, if you want, so they don't have to go out of their way."

She looks over her shoulder and back to me. "Okay. I'll tell Dad and grab my bag. I'll be right back."

I release her hand and watch as she hurries back inside.

When she reemerges, she is wrapped in her red coat, and her purse is in her hand.

I open the passenger door and shut it quietly so as not to wake Cobie. Then, I drive her into town.

Pulling the SUV up to the flower shop, I leave it running while I walk her the five steps to the door. I take her keys from her and unlock the dead bolt.

"Thank you," she says as I hand them back.

I glance at the SUV to make sure Cobie is still sleeping, and then I take Sela's face into my hands.

"I shouldn't have taken off like I did this morning. I—shit, I didn't know what to say. I really enjoyed our night, and I should have woken you to say good-bye," I confess.

Her hand comes up and clasps my wrist. "It's okay."

Her eyes glisten, and I feel like an asshole.

"No, it isn't. I'm so sorry."

I press my forehead to hers.

"You're forgiven," she murmurs.

I lift her face and bring her lips to mine. I kiss her softly.

"Good night, Sela."

"Sweet dreams," she whispers.

I move aside and hold the door open for her.

"Lock it when you get inside," I command.

She steps into the flower shop and immediately engages the dead bolt. Then, she waves before disappearing into the darkened shop.

I will definitely be having sweet dreams tonight.

Chapter Nineteen

Sela

THE LAST FEW DAYS HAVE BEEN A BLUR OF ACTIVITY. THE MAYOR and I had meetings with two separate groups of private investors who are interested in the museum project, and I've pulled a couple of late nights, working on proposals for each of them to consider.

Today, Dawn is coming in for an overview of the town's lake conservation efforts, so I put together a PowerPoint presentation and arranged for lunch to be catered in from the café.

The two of us settle into the conference room, and I click through the slideshow on the screen as she follows along in the portfolio I printed for her.

"So, you guys close the lake every spring to dredge it? Why?" she asks.

"Dredging helps us control the lake's environment by removing trash, sludge, dead vegetation, and other debris. It keeps the water clean for swimming, and it preserves the local wildlife's ecosystems. It also helps reverse eutrophication," I explain.

"Eutrophi what?" she asks.

"Eutrophication. It's an excess of nutrients in the water due to runoff."

"And that's a bad thing?"

I nod. "It causes a dense growth of plant life, and that can lead to the loss of animal life due to lack of oxygen."

She looks from her papers to the screen. "This says that one of the risks of dredging is lowering oxygen levels and releasing harmful chemicals," she points out.

"That's correct. If it's done incorrectly, it can also damage fish spawning grounds and even make the banks unstable. It's a delicate balance, and we take it very seriously. That's why we have a Lake Conservation Society. It raises funds so that the town can afford to consciously dredge, which not only protects the ecosystems, but also clears settlement to increase the depths of the navigation channels, ensuring the safe passage of boats. That provides a good fishing environment, which brings in tourism during the spring and summer months and funds the conservation efforts."

"I see," she says as she writes down a few notes. "And you say the lake is safe for swimming?"

"Technically, but we don't employ lifeguards, and there are snakes and other hazards, so we encourage visitors to make use of the community pool instead. We also have the swimming hole on the other side of the dam, and it's clear and shallow, so camping families do take advantage of it during the summer."

"Interesting. So, Lake Mistletoe isn't just a place to visit in December," she surmises.

"Granted, the holidays are the best time of year here, but we have a lot to offer year-round. With Bran and Dad opening up the new zip line adventure next year, we forecast an influx of summer and early fall vacationers."

"Well, I'm sold. I think Daniel and I will be spending more time here. Maybe we'll even buy a little cabin in the woods or something," she says as she stands.

I flick the overhead lights to life and turn off the screen.

"We'd love to have you guys," I tell her.

Roxie arrives with our lunch, and we switch from professional mode to girlfriend mode.

"It's nice that Isaac and Cobie are still in town," she says as she dresses her salad.

"Yeah, he'll be able to capture many more of the town's activities leading up to Christmas," I muse.

She nods. "That will come in handy for my article. Plus, you can steal a few more kisses before he leaves," she says.

I blink up from my plate to look at her.

"Don't give me that look," she quips.

"I have no idea what you're talking about," I reply.

"Cobie already filled me in on your little smooch under the mistletoe. And I was there at the concert when you two swapped spit on the dance floor, remember?"

I open my mouth to respond and then close it. What can I say?

"Uh-huh. I thought so," she cracks.

I shrug. "He's a good kisser."

"I bet he is," she remarks.

"Am I crazy for even entertaining any kind of relationship with him?" I ask.

She puts her fork down and looks at me. "Isaac's a good guy. He and his wife weren't suited for each other, but they communicate and are otherwise amicable co-parents. He's handsome. Has a lucrative career. Basically, he's a catch," she claims.

"He's also a vagabond who stays on the road most of the time," I state.

"That's true, but that can be fun. Imagine exploring the world with him."

That does sound nice.

"I have dreams that include being right here and running a museum," I say.

"You can have roots and wings. It doesn't have to be one or the other. You just have to compromise," she insists.

True.

I shake my head. "It's a moot point. A few stolen kisses don't amount to any type of commitment. We're just enjoying each other while he's here," I inform her.

"If you say so."

When the workday is finished, I swing by my apartment and change into a comfy pair of jeans and a cozy sweater before Norah drives us to the inn to help Hannah set the tables up for the shower.

Isaac is outside, watching Cobie and Lexie as they sled down the hill at the side of the inn, a pensive smile curling his lips.

"Hiya, handsome," I say as I approach, pulling him from his thoughts.

"Hi, yourself," he says.

"Any luck with the birth certificates?" I ask.

He shakes his head. "Lonnie sent Cobie's, but she didn't have a copy of mine. She requested a copy from the local courthouse in Texas, but she was declined because we are divorced. I went online and requested a copy be sent to her address since I'm not there to request it in person, but that could take up to thirty days."

"So, Europe isn't going to happen?" I ask.

"Not unless our passports magically appear in the next few days."

"It doesn't seem like it should be so hard," I say.

His eyes cut to me. "It shouldn't be."

"My mom always says that God will create roadblocks to protect you from unseen trouble. Maybe it's a blessing that you're stuck here," I console.

The corner of his mouth rises in a half-smile. "Maybe."

We walk inside and follow the scent of fresh ginger and nutmeg, finding Trixie and Alice in the kitchen.

"What's going on in here?" I ask as I survey the cookie sheets set on cooling racks.

"Isaac here inspired us," Trixie replies.

"I did?" Isaac asks.

"Yes, with your Swedish porridge demonstration the other night. We decided that we'd like to make some treats from around the world, so we asked some of the guests if they had any requests. Mr. Fritz said his German grandmother used to make him pfeffernusse cookies every Christmas when he was a kid. He hasn't had one since she passed over two decades ago, so I found a recipe. The only ingredients we didn't have in the pantry were the star anise and blackstrap molasses, but I sent Bob to the market. Oh, and just for you, Isaac, we made a batch of peppermint buttercream-filled macarons. We'll serve them after dinner tonight," Alice expounds.

"What about the gingerbread theme?" Isaac asks.

"We'll have gingerbread bread pudding as well," Trixie replies.

He reaches for one of the pink-hued cookie sandwiches that are cooling.

Alice smacks at his hand.

"Oh, no, you don't. No spoiling your dinner. Now, get out of my kitchen." She shoos us away.

"I'd better get back out there and make sure Cobie and Lexie don't break a leg," he says as we stand in the hallway.

"The girls are waiting on me in the atrium," I say.

"Are you staying for dinner?" he asks.

"I can."

He smiles. "Then, I'll see you soon."

He walks off toward the front of the inn. I make my way to the back door and out to the atrium, where Hannah and Norah are already draping the round tables—which Keller and Bran set up around the garden—with tablecloths.

I dive right in and get to work, prepping the food stations and making signs to label each dish. I make a mental note to ask Willa's favorite punch flavor as I set the crystal punch bowl in the center of the sweets table.

Hannah, ever the organized one, starts creating a checklist, ensuring we don't miss a single detail.

As we work, laughter and chatter fill the garden, reflecting the joy we're putting into every aspect of this celebration for our friend, because we're not just planning a baby shower; we're weaving memories into every decoration, every centerpiece, making sure that Willa feels the love and excitement we have for her and Keller's growing family.

When we are done, I can't help but imagine Willa's face lighting up when she enters the venue, greeted by the baby safari wonderland we've meticulously crafted.

This baby shower isn't just about celebrating a new life; it's about creating a magical moment that Willa will cherish forever.

"I think that's it, ladies," Norah says as she loops an arm around both our necks.

"It's perfect," Hannah whispers.

"Yep, and Willa is going to love it. We just have to ensure that she doesn't sneak a peek before Friday," I add.

Norah grins. "Not a problem. I threatened her."

"She can literally see into the atrium every time she walks from her home to the inn," I point out.

"It's two days. Surely, she can resist for two days," Hannah mutters.

"I'd better enlist Keller's help," Norah says.

The back door opens, and Willa's voice calls out, "Dinner's ready!"

"Don't come out here!"

We all three begin shouting at once as we rush toward her.

Chapter Twenty

Isaac

AFTER DINNER, COBIE AND LEXIE CHANGE INTO THEIR PAJAMAS and snuggle together in Lexie's room to watch television. Cobie has spent the last few nights sleeping in here since we moved next door into Alice and Hal's room.

I guess it's more fun to share a room with your friend than your father.

"You want to take a walk with me?" I ask Sela after helping get the girls settled.

"Sure."

I grab my coat and my camera and meet her at the front door.

Sela bundles up in her coat and matching hat, gloves, and scarf.

"Where are we going?" she asks as we step out into the chilly night air.

"I wanted to get a few shots of the lake and the bridge at night," I tell her.

"You already got photos of the bridge," she reminds me.

"I know, but it was crowded with other elf hunters that night. I'd like to get some tranquil snaps of the lights reflecting in the water with the mountains in the background," I explain.

We walk side by side across the street and down the sidewalk. The glow from the lampposts illuminate her face as snowflakes gather in her hair that is peeking beneath her hat.

I reach for her hand as we fall into step together.

When we arrive at the bridge, I let go of her and take my camera in hand, the chill of the snowy mountainside biting through my gloves. My breath mingles with the frosty air as I adjust the lens and point it in her direction.

"I thought you wanted photos without people in them."

"People, no. Just you," I say.

She shakes her head as I click the button, and the flash highlights her figure against the vast expanse of the dark waters.

Suddenly, movement catches my eye. A massive moose, its antlers crowned with snow, stands proudly against the white backdrop of the lake's bank behind her.

"Sela, look," I whisper as I lift my chin over her shoulder.

She turns and gasps. "Oh my goodness, look at him."

I take her hand and lead her across the bridge so I can get a better angle.

With silent steps, we approach the majestic creature, careful not to startle it.

I raise my camera, fingers steady despite the cold.

Click.

The shutter captures the moose's regal presence, its eyes reflecting both curiosity and alertness.

"It's okay, big fella. We won't hurt you," I whisper.

Sela stands beside me, quiet as a mouse.

Time seems to stand still as we observe the moose, its powerful form in contrast with the pristine snow—a living testament to the wild beauty of the mountains.

I continue snapping pictures of the graceful animal as it turns to head back into the cover of the forest, its movements deliberate yet elegant. The snowflakes dance around it, adding a touch of magic to the tranquil moment.

"This place is something else," I mutter as the moose disappears into the trees.

Sela's arms snake around me, and her chin rests on my shoulder.

I can feel her body shiver against my back.

"I should get you back inside," I say.

She nods, and I turn and tug her close to my side as I guide us back onto the path that leads back to the way we came.

All is dark and quiet when we step back into the inn. Everyone has retired for the night.

"Looks like my ride left me," Sela quips.

I offer to take her home, and this time, I pack an overnight bag before leading her to the SUV.

Just in case.

We park in the lot across from her place and hurry inside.

She locks the door and flips the switch on the wall.

Nothing.

She flicks it up and down a few times before walking to the kitch-enette and trying the door to the refrigerator.

No light.

"Great. The power's out," she says.

The temperature outside is falling, but her apartment is still warm.

"It must not have been out long," I say as I remove my coat and toss it on the sofa.

"Is that usable?" I ask as I assess the black iron woodstove that is nestled in the corner of the room.

"Yes, I've only used it once, but I have a small supply of firewood in the closet," she says.

I take my phone and turn the flashlight function on. Then, I bend to my knee so I can look inside the stove and open the damper as Sela gathers an armload of wood.

I take it from her and stack it inside.

Sela brings me a furniture catalog from her nightstand, and I rip pages out, crumple them into a ball, and arrange them around and under the wood.

Sela sets candles around the room and lights them with a box of matches she fished out of a kitchen drawer. Then, she passes the box to me, and I strike a match to light the kindling.

Once the fire is crackling, she pulls the comforter from her bed and carries it to the rug that lies between the stove and the sofa. She spreads it out and places cushions from the back of the sofa against the ottoman. She grabs another blanket from the closet and the pillows from her bed, and we settle in front of the fire.

I fall onto my back as I watch the flames dance through the opening, and Sela cuddles into my side.

"What do we do now?" she asks.

"We can spoon."

"Okay. I like to be the big spoon though," she declares.

I look down at her tiny frame and grin.

"And how would that work exactly?" I ask.

"Like this." She pushes me to my side and throws a leg over me as she snuggles into my back.

We lie in silence as she begins rubbing circles over the ribs under my arm.

She leans her face into my throat, and I feel her lips move to the spot below my ear. Her warm breath washes over me, causing my skin to prickle. I close my eyes as she peppers kisses down the back of my neck to my shoulder blade.

She feeds her knee over my hip, using her weight to bring me to my back, and slides on top of me, chest to chest.

My arms come around her as she crawls up my body until we are nose to nose.

"Can you stay the night?" she asks against my mouth.

"I planned on it," I answer.

She grins.

One minute, she's on top, and the next, I have her on her back, pinned to the floor.

I nuzzle her neck and graze her earlobe with my teeth. She shudders.

"Oh, you like that?" I ask as I nibble at her ear again.

She moans her approval.

"And now?" I whisper as I suck her earlobe into my mouth.

"Getting better," she answers breathlessly.

I bring my mouth to hers and nip at her bottom lip. She sighs, and my tongue dips in to taste her.

This kiss is different than before. It's not soft or sweet. It's demanding and wanting, and I feel it all the way to my toes.

She laces her hands into my hair and holds on.

Needy little noises bubble up from her throat as she claws at the hem of my shirt.

I don't think anyone has ever kissed me so thoroughly, her urgency setting my body on fire.

"And now?" I ask as I break the kiss and lift my head to look into her eyes.

"I like it," she whimpers.

I lean back on my thighs and let her tug my shirt free from my jeans. She fumbles with the buttons, and once it's open, her mouth finds my chest.

She runs her hands over my sides and around to my back. I let her explore my skin as I grow hard above her.

161

When she starts to slowly move her hips against me, finding friction where she needs it most, I groan.

It's a deep, guttural sound that lets her know I want this as badly as she does.

One second, her tongue is climbing the column of my throat as she writhes beneath me. The next, I'm on my feet.

"What are you doing?" she asks breathlessly.

"Getting you naked, " I growl as I strip her leggings and sweater and toss them aside before slowly crawling back up her body and kissing her again.

She wraps her legs around me, and I pull my cock free from my jeans. It's hard and ready against the silk of her panties.

I take a finger and tug aside the cup of her bra so my mouth can reach her breast. As I take a nipple between my teeth and gently bite down, she cries out my name.

She plants her feet, raises her hips off the ground, and circles them.

Oh, yes, sweet contact.

I don't think I've ever been this turned on before. My body is coiled tight and screaming for release.

She trembles beneath me, and I sit up on my knees.

She moans her displeasure.

I chuckle.

"So impatient," I say as I hook my fingers into the sides of her panties and slowly slide the silk barrier down her thighs.

Her legs fall open.

I sit there, looking down at her reverently. She's totally exposed to me and so damn ready.

I glide a finger through her wetness before I kick my jeans off. I slide on a condom and come back on top of her.

She rakes her fingernails down my back as I find her entrance and slowly move inside.

"Finally," she gasps.

Stranded in Lake Mistletoe

We keep a slow-building pace. Her eyes never leave mine—until my control snaps and I can no longer hold back. She locks her knees to my sides as my hips drive urgently in and out.

She rises to meet my thrusts as I try to hold off the burning sensation that's crawling up my spine. Sweat beads at my brow as I cling to the thread of control until an explosion of pleasure sweeps her up. She scores her nails down my back as she dives off the cliff, and I cover her mouth with mine to swallow her muffled cries until she is panting and sated.

Then, I let go and follow her into the deep end.

Chapter Twenty-One

Sela

A BEEPING NOISE DRAGS ME FROM A GLORIOUS DREAM. I roll to the side and hit something hard and warm. Opening one eye, I look up into Isaac's amused face.

"Good morning, sleepyhead," he says.

"You're still here," I rasp.

His hand comes up and sweeps my hair behind my ear. "Yep. Although I do need to head back to the inn before Cobie misses me," he says.

I sit up and look around the room. "What is that noise?" I ask.

"I think it's your phone's alarm," he replies.

"What time is it?"

He leans forward, snags his jeans from the floor, and finds his phone. "Seven."

I raise my arms above me and stretch, but Isaac grabs my wrist and twists to pin me to the pillow.

"You want to come have breakfast with us?" he asks as he kisses my neck.

"Mmm, I wish I could, but I have a meeting with the mayor in an hour, and then I'm taking Dawn to the ice-skating rink," I tell him as my eyes flutter close, and I enjoy the feel of his tongue on my skin.

"Ice skating," he repeats.

"Yep. You want to meet us? You can bring Cobie, and I can snap some photos of you on the ice," I suggest.

He shakes his head. "I document the story. I'm not a part of the story."

"That's sad. What would happen if you did become part of it?" I ask.

He lifts his head. "I have no idea. I've never wanted to be part of it before."

I wrap my arms around his neck and pull his mouth to mine.

He kisses me, and I don't even care that I haven't brushed my teeth yet this morning. I just want his lips on mine.

He groans.

"I should go," he says as he continues to pepper my lips, cheeks, and nose with kisses.

"Me too," I murmur.

He rolls off of me and stands to pull his jeans on.

I do the same and slide into my sweater before following him to the door.

"I'm supposed to help your brother take the globe to the garage tonight," he says.

"I have to be at a Christmas dinner the mayor and his wife are hosting for council members," I say.

"So, I'll see you tomorrow?" he asks.

"Yep, I'll be at the inn for the baby shower," I inform him.

"I'll see you then," he says before giving me one more peck on the lips.

"See you then," I agree.

He disappears down the stairs, and I shut the door behind him.

Oh my, I'm going to be late.

I hurry into the office to prep for the meeting.

"Late again. I'm going to need details," Roxie sings as I rush past her desk.

After a brief meeting to go over the schedule of events for this weekend's tree lighting and boat parade, I leave town hall and walk the short distance to the ice rink.

Dawn and her husband are already sitting at a bench, lacing up their skates, when I arrive.

"Sela," she calls as she waves me over.

"I'm just going to grab a pair of skates. Be right there," I shout back.

I get in line with the other customers to give the clerk my shoe size. He exchanges my heels for a pair of well-worn blades, and I join Dawn.

"I haven't been on ice skates since I was little," she says as she waits for me to slide into my pair.

Daniel is already on the ice, gliding effortlessly around the rink, practically dancing to the Christmas music pumping through the speakers as he dodges the other skaters.

"It's like riding a bike," I encourage as we stand. "Daniel seems to have it down pat," I muse.

Her eyes find him among the crowd, and she rolls them. "Blah, I swear he's good at everything."

I laugh. "Sounds like a good trait to have," I quip.

"I guess it's kinda hot until he leaves me on my own to break my neck," she says as she clutches my hand tightly.

I lead her to the ice, and I turn so that I'm facing her as I take both her hands. I glide backward at a slow pace as I fight to keep us both upright.

"Relax. You're doing great," I encourage her.

"Liar. I'm about to take us both out, along with a few kiddos," she says.

"Stop looking down at your feet. Look at me," I command.

She squeezes my fingers harder as she does as instructed.

"There you go now, just let me lead."

We make several successful laps when Daniel starts to whistle from the sideline.

When we make it to him, he skates out to us.

"I got her," he says as he relieves me of her grasp.

I move to the outside of the rink and kick my feet to gain speed. Then, I move to the middle and throw myself into a spin.

Cheering sounds from the left side of the rink, and I open my eyes and search the fence line.

Isaac and Cobie are standing there. She is calling my name and waving while he has his face behind his camera.

"Do it again," Cobie shouts.

I make another lap and then take off into an upright spin, ending in a sitting spin.

Cobie screams as I stand and take a bow.

The flash from Isaac's camera goes off above her head.

Dawn stumbles up beside me. "That was awesome," she squeals as she latches on to my arm.

"You live here long enough, and you pick up a few tricks," I tell her as I lead us back to the bench.

"I'm going to practice so I can come back next year and we can spend an entire day skating," she promises.

"I'd love that."

Cobie comes flying around the building that houses the skate rentals.

"Sela, can you teach me how to spin?" she gasps as she comes to a screeching halt.

Isaac is on her heels. "Not today, Cobie. We just stopped so I could take some pictures of Dawn and Sela. We're on our way to work on the boat," he reminds her.

She grimaces. "Oh yeah."

I smile at her. "I'll teach you some spins before you have to go home," I promise.

"Tomorrow?" she asks.

"We have the baby shower after work tomorrow, but we can make time after the Christmas Market this weekend."

Her face lights up. "It's a date," she bellows.

She gives Dawn, Daniel, and me hugs before taking Isaac's hand and following him out of the skating area.

Dawn and I hand our skates to Daniel, and he goes to retrieve our shoes.

"What's next on the agenda?" she asks.

I smirk. "Food and wine."

Chapter Twenty-Two

Isaac

"I THINK WE'RE DONE," BRAN SAYS AS WE STAND BACK TO ADMIRE the work.

There was a small hiccup when we lowered the sphere onto the rotating platform. The weight of the glass caused the belt on the wheel to jam. We had to remove it and reconfigure the pulley, using a bicycle chain and a slightly bigger motor.

The crest of the dome stands seven feet tall. Bran affixed a hook to the top, and Hannah crafted a faux sprig of mistletoe, using leaves from a fake banana plant and white Christmas ornaments for berries. The scene that Bran painted on the sides of the kayaks serves as the ideal base for the snow globe, and the speaker system I installed is hidden perfectly within the bow and stern of the vessels. A wireless microphone is programmed into the speakers so Bran can talk to the crowd above the sound of the music.

I clap him on the back. "I believe you have a winner," I tell him.

He nods. "Even if I don't win the ribbon," he agrees.

"Should we test it out before tomorrow?" I ask. The thought of us launching it into the water and it immediately sinking flashes in my mind.

He shakes his head. "Nope. I don't want to risk anyone seeing it or us breaking the globe. We're just going to have to have faith," he says.

"It'll float just fine," Norris assures. "Let's throw a tarp on her and head out."

Hannah called earlier and informed us that Keller requested our help with breaking down tables and hauling the baby shower loot and the crib up to the nursery.

We cover the boat, and Bran drives us to the inn.

The driveway is full, and we have to park down the street. It seems that the entire town showed up to celebrate Willa's little one.

Hannah meets us at the door, followed by a woman I don't recognize.

"The party isn't quite over yet. We have one more game to play, and then I'll hand out the favors," Hannah informs us.

"Is there any food left?" Norris asks.

"Plenty. You guys can help yourselves once the guests leave," she says.

"Perfect. I'll be watching the television. Just holler when you're ready for us," Norris announces before walking inside.

"Isaac, this is my mother, Trudy. She came in early for the shower and will be staying with Aunt Trixie through the new year," Hannah introduces.

"It's nice to meet you," I greet.

"Oh, you are handsome," she says as she takes my offered hand.

"Mom," Hannah says under her breath.

"I mean, it's nice to meet you too, Isaac. Your daughter is lovely."

"Thank you."

She releases me and gives Bran a warm hug.

"Come on, Mom. We'd better get back to the party," Hannah says.

She goes up on her tiptoes and kisses Bran, and then the two of them hurry back to the garden.

We go in search of Keller and find him and Bob sitting with Norris in the great room.

The five of us sit and watch Utah play USC in the Pac-12 championship game until Trixie calls for us a little over an hour later.

Cobie runs to me when I step out into the atrium.

"Daddy, I won a prize," she shouts, holding up a basket containing a selection of cocoa mixes, colorful marshmallow packets, and a dainty pink-and-gold mug, saucer, and spoon.

"That's nice," I tell her.

She explains that she played musical chairs, and when the music stopped, she sat on a balloon that popped, and there was a little plastic baby inside.

She shows me the baby that she has tucked into the basket.

"Sounds like you had a lot of fun," I say.

"It was the best. Can Lexie and I make cocoa?" she asks.

"How about we save that for after dinner tonight?" I suggest.

"Okay," she agrees without argument. "Can I video Mommy and show her my basket?"

"Sure. Do you remember how the video works?" I ask.

She nods, and I hand her my phone.

I spot Sela standing by the punch bowl. She's wearing a cream-colored sweater dress and a pair of knee-high, heeled leather boots.

"Did you win any prizes?" I ask as I approach her.

"Unfortunately, no," she replies.

"I like this," I say as I tug the side of her dress.

"You do?"

"Yep, it hugs your curves in all the right places," I growl.

Her eyes flare with heat.

"And those boots are sexy as hell."

A throat clears, and I glance over my shoulder to see Norris standing there.

Shit.

I step away from his daughter as his assessing eyes dart between the two of us.

"Hi, Daddy," she says.

"Sweetheart, you look beautiful," he says as he pulls her into a warm hug.

"You guys are going to give me a big head," she says as she returns his embrace.

"The truth is the truth," he states. Then, he leans in and asks, "Can you point me toward the food?"

Sela steps aside and points him in the direction of the catering table.

"Don't look so guilty," she whispers as we watch him make his way to the leftovers.

"I'm not used to a father sneaking up on me while I'm trying to make his daughter blush," I say.

She pops me in the chest. "That's what you were doing!"

I chuckle. "Yep, because the only thing sexier than those boots is when your cheeks turn pink and I know you're thinking something dirty," I murmur in her ear.

She giggles. "You're bad."

"Hey, lover boy, can we get a little help over here?"

I turn to see Bran and Keller balancing the ends of the crib as they carry it toward the steps that lead up to Keller and Willa's home.

"Coming," I call. "I'd better go before they break their necks," I tell her.

"Good idea."

I walk backward, not taking my eyes off her.

She shakes her head as the pink finally creeps up her neck and hits her cheeks.

There it is.

I wink at her before I turn and navigate the guys up to the nursery.

Chapter Twenty-Three

Sela

TODAY'S THE DAY. MY FAVORITE OF THE ENTIRE YEAR.

I wake early, shower, and dress in a warm Christmas sweater and fleece-lined leggings before heading downstairs.

Norah and her sister, Donna, are in the shop. Barry, Donna's husband, is loading the bed of his truck with poinsettias and potted miniature Christmas trees to haul to the flower shop booth at the market.

"Sela, will you be my partner in the reindeer games? Donna here is claiming her ankle hurts to get out of it." Norah scowls.

"My ankle is hurt," Donna defends as she raises her pants leg to reveal a swollen purple area above the sock covering her right foot.

"Whatever," Norah says.

"Um, I'm supposed to show Dawn and Isaac around for the mayor," I inform her.

"So? You can still participate," Norah says.

"Why can't Sammy be your partner?" Donna asks.

"Because he has the coordination of a newborn calf—that's why."

Donna rolls her eyes. "God, you're so competitive. It's like Pop and Keller and the boat contest."

"And you are a big fat letdowner," Norah retorts.

I throw my hand up. "Don't fight. I'll do it," I relent.

Donna's eyes flicker to me. "Good luck partnering with this one. She is worse than my kids."

Norah sticks her tongue out at her sister as Donna hobbles out of the door and to Barry's truck.

"How fast are you at wrapping?" Norah asks.

I shrug. "Average."

She shakes her head. "I'm gonna kill Donna for getting hurt."

"Can you give me a ride to The Gingerbread Inn?" I ask.

"Sure."

"When does the boat parade start?" Cobie asks as I lead her and her father through the throngs of festivalgoers.

"Just past sunset. The mayor will light the Christmas tree first, and then he'll call for all the contestants to bring their boats to the shore," I tell her.

"How long is it until sunset?"

"Several hours," Isaac replies.

"Darn it," she grumbles.

I squeeze her hand. "Don't worry; there are lots of things to enjoy before then," I say.

Her curious eyes come to mine. "Like what?"

"First off are the reindeer games," I say.

"What's that?" she asks.

"Do you have a field day at school?" I ask.

She shakes her head. "No, but my mommy took me to watch our neighbors at their field day."

"Okay, the reindeer games are like field day. You pick a partner, and the two of you compete against other teams of two in a bunch of holiday-themed races for a prize. I signed you and your dad up to play," I explain.

She glances back at Isaac. "Daddy, you have to try really hard, and you can't take pictures," she commands.

"Not even one picture?" he asks.

She sticks up her index finger. "One. But only if it's not our turn."

"You got it, boss," he says.

I guide them through the tents, where we sample the offered wares. People are milling about, chatting joyfully, and children have their faces painted, like reindeer or elves, and eat all the sugary holiday treats they can manage.

Isaac stealthily leads us under every single mistletoe he spots and kisses us both each time while Cobie giggles.

When we find ourselves surrounded by Dickens-costumed carolers, we sing along.

"*Deck the halls with balls of holly. Fa-la-la-la-la,*" Isaac's booming baritone sings.

"Did you just say, *deck the halls with* balls *of holly?*" I ask.

"Yes, that's what the song says."

"No, the song says *boughs* of holly," I correct.

"What the heck is a bough?" he asks.

"It's another way to say branch. Like a branch from a holly bush. People confuse it for mistletoe," I explain.

Isaac's brows furrow. "Really? I like balls," he says.

"Me too," Cobie says.

I spit apple cider, and it sprays across the carolers.

"Oh." I cover my mouth as I mutter, "I'm so sorry."

They give me a disapproving look and continue their mission of spreading Christmas cheer through the crowd.

Cobie spots Lexie with her parents and takes off to greet her friend.

"Christmas field day, huh?" Isaac says as he falls into step beside me.

"That's right. A wreath race, timed gift wrapping, Christmas limbo, pin the tail on Rudolph." I name a few of the games.

"And you signed me up for this?" he asks.

"I sure did. If I have to participate as Norah's partner, you have to suffer too."

"That's just mean," he accuses.

I laugh.

"Dawn and Daniel signed up, and I thought Cobie would enjoy doing it with you," I clarify.

"Hopefully, I don't fall on my face and cost her a stuffed snowman or something equally valuable," he says.

"I promise not to laugh if you do."

"I appreciate that," he says.

We find Dawn and Daniel waiting in line at the roasted chestnut cart, and they join us as we take Cobie to visit Santa, who is sitting in the sleigh that Keller and Bran made for him.

We wait for our turn, and Isaac takes photos as Cobie climbs the steps of the sleigh and takes a seat beside the realistic-looking Santa.

They talk in low voices before an elf helps her down the other side to where Dawn, Daniel, and I are waiting and sends her off with a candy cane.

Isaac snaps a couple more frames before he rounds the front to join us.

"What about you, young fella?" Santa calls.

I look up to see who he's shouting at.

He looks right at Isaac and nods. "Yes, you there with the camera. What do you want for Christmas this year, Isaac?" he asks as he points his white-glove-covered finger at him.

"How do you know—" Isaac begins.

"Your name? Haven't you heard? I know everybody," he answers the unfinished question.

Isaac grins.

"A million dollars," he quips.

Santa's brows drop, as if Isaac's answer disappoints him.

"Can't you come up with anything better than that?" he asks.

Better than a million dollars?

"You wouldn't happen to know where our passports are?" Isaac asks.

He smiles. "I'd guess they are right where they're supposed to be," he replies cryptically.

"No, sir, they're not. That's why I asked you," Isaac retorts.

Santa belly-laughs, and I swear it sounds like, "Ho, ho, ho," as it floats down from his perch above us.

He waves over the next child in line, and Isaac shake his head as if to clear it of the strange exchange when the mayor's voice sounds over the intercom system, calling all reindeer game contestants to meet by the Christmas tree.

Once we've all gathered, he announces the first competition. The three-legged wreath race.

We line up in the bustling heart of the Christmas Market. Norah and me, Isaac and Cobie, Dawn and Daniel, and a few other pairs. We start side by side, our legs expertly bound together by Hal with a festive wreath.

Isaac grins down at his daughter, his eyes twinkling with a mix of determination and playful mischief. "Ready, Cobie? Let's show these guys what we're made of," he shouts.

"Yeah, we're gonna take you guys down," Cobie tells Norah.

"A little shit-talker, I see," Norah mumbles under her breath.

I elbow her in the side, and she grunts.

Cobie's small hand grips the wreath tightly, mirroring Isaac's firm hold.

Hoyt's voice booms through the market, declaring the start of the race.

With synchronized movements, Isaac and Cobie surge forward, their laughter harmonizing with the jingle of the bells on their wreath.

The crowd cheers them on as Cobie's ponytail bobs with each stride, but Norah and I are close on their heels.

Dodging our way through the maze of market stalls, Norah wills us to pass the father-daughter team.

Cobie's eyes sparkle with excitement as Isaac shouts uplifting words, pushing her to go faster.

As we approach a tricky turn, Cobie stumbles slightly, but Isaac's strong grip steadies her.

"You're doing great, Cobie! Keep going!" I cheer.

"Whose side are you on?" Norah snaps as we power through the turn.

The race continues, each step bringing us closer to the finish line.

The market seems to blur around us as we focus solely on our goal.

With the finish line in sight, Cobie's energy begins to waver.

The crowd roars with encouragement, urging her forward.

In a burst of speed, wreath still intact, they cross the finish line half a beat before us and nearly two whole minutes before a fumbling Dawn and Daniel.

Breathless and beaming, Cobie hugs her father tightly, their laughter blending with the joyful cacophony of the market.

At that moment, they are a team, and as they catch their breath, Isaac ruffles Cobie's hair affectionately.

"We did it, Cobie. We make a great team," he praises.

Cobie beams up at him, her eyes shining with pride and love. "The best team, Daddy."

It's the only one they win as we move through the rest of the games, but it doesn't matter. Watching Cobie fumble with wrapping paper and tape and Isaac repeatedly falling on his bum during a spirited game of limbo as his daughter shrieks with joy is reward enough.

Chapter Twenty-Four

Isaac

THE SUN BEGINS TO SET, AND WE WEAVE OUR WAY THROUGH the crowd toward the tall blue spruce on the side of the lake.

We gather around as the moon rises in the night sky. I hoist Cobie onto my shoulders so she has a bird's-eye view as Hoyt leads us in a countdown.

"Ten, nine, eight, seven, six, five, four, three, two, one!" He takes the silver arm and flips it.

The branches come to life as a thousand lights begin to blink awake.

Cobie screams her delight as the crowd erupts in cheers.

The intercom announces that the contestants with boat parade entries need to meet at the launch pad, so I set Cobie on her feet. She takes Sela's hand, and I follow Bran, Hannah, and Norris.

"Good luck, Daddy," Cobie calls after us.

We get the boat to the water's edge, and Norris holds on to the ropes as Bran helps Hannah up the ramp and onto the platform.

Once everything is set, I climb into the seat at the front of one of the kayaks with my camera bag slung across my shoulder. Norris pushes off of the bank and takes a seat at the rear on the opposite side. We both grab the oars that are tucked in the body of the kayaks and start to row out into the lake as the other boats launch.

When we reach the center of the bridge, we bring in the oars and wait.

When the last boat hits the water, I start the turntable and the snow machine. The two of them start to rotate under the mistletoe, and I press the button for the lights that frame the base and the spot-light that illuminates the couple. Then, Norris starts the music.

Bran and Hannah hold hands and press their lips together as the snow swirls around them, and she raises a leg in the air.

I take my camera from its bag and focus on the two of them, and the crowd rejoices as they take in the scene.

As we all take a lap toward the bank, Hoyt assigns numbers to each boat and instructs the crowd how to vote for their favorite.

Just as Hoyt is about to call for the boats to come back in, Bran's voice pierces the air, asking for everyone's attention.

Hannah's confusion is evident as the music softens, and Bran slowly goes to a knee.

"Hannah Whitmar, you came barreling into my life a year ago and literally knocked me off my feet," he begins as she lets out a sobbing laugh. "I want every year of my life to be as crazy and happy as this one was, and I know as long as I wake up to you every morning, it will be."

He pulls the black velvet box from his pocket and opens the top to reveal an exquisite pear-shaped diamond ring. Hannah sucks in a breath, and her hand goes to her heart.

A hush falls over the masses.

"Will you marry me? Please," he continues, his voice cracking on the last word.

I focus my lens on her face. The words are stuck in her throat as the tears stream down her cheeks.

"Baby?" he whispers.

She starts nodding her head as she extends her left hand to him.

"I need the words, Hannah," he coaxes.

"Yes, yes, yes, I'll marry you," she bellows.

Bran places the ring on her finger and stands to his feet so fast that it jolts the kayaks, and I nearly lose my camera to the lake.

He picks her up, and her head sends one of the white ornaments hanging from the mistletoe crashing to the platform as he kisses her senseless.

The crowd erupts in cheers and applause as the rest of the boats make their way back to the bank.

Norris and I take our time rowing our vessel in, letting the couple inside savor the moment.

When we reach the others, all of their friends and family are waiting to greet them.

The women all embrace Hannah and gush over the ring while the men shake Bran's hand.

It's a beautiful scene. One I capture for my new friends.

Keller and Bob wade through the well-wishers, and Keller gives Bran a scathing look.

"You pulled a fast one."

Bran grins at him and shrugs.

Keller chuckles. "I couldn't be happier to take second place, but enjoy it because, next year, that blue ribbon is coming home."

Hoyt officially announces the winner, and Bran proudly lifts the ribbon into the air.

Then, he reminds the boys and girls in the audience that Santa is watching and that they need to behave if they want to stay off his naughty list.

Trudy and Trixie, who were also in on the plan, move the celebration to the inn, where they have set up refreshments in the garden.

I find Sela and Cobie at the foot of the Christmas tree.

"There're my girls. Are you two ready to head back to the inn?" I ask.

Sela turns her concerned eyes to me. Her hand is resting on Cobie's shoulder.

"What's wrong?" I ask as I hurry to their side.

"I don't know. She just started crying out of nowhere, and I can't console her," Sela says.

I crouch to her eye level and take her face into my hands. "Talk to me, baby girl. What's going on? Are you hurt?"

She gasps for air as she tries to tell me.

"Slow down. Take a couple of breaths," I tell her.

She falls into my arms, her wet cheek coming to rest against my neck.

I pick her up and stand, rubbing soothing circles on her back.

Panic fills every fiber of my being as I hold my wailing daughter in my arms.

Once her body goes limp and her sobs turn to whimpers, I walk us to a bench by the lake and sit her in my lap.

I wipe the tears from under her eyes and wait for her to pull herself together.

"I did a bad thing, and Santa isn't going to forgive me," she explains between hiccups.

"I don't think there's anything that Santa can't forgive if you confess, offer a sincere apology, and ask for forgiveness," I tell her.

"But what if I'm not sorry?" she asks.

"You're not sorry for doing the bad thing?"

She shakes her head.

"I'm afraid I'm going to need a little more information before I can help," I say.

Her bottom lip quivers, and it breaks my heart to see her in such emotional turmoil.

"I did it," she whispers.

"Did what?"

"I took the bag from your suitcase and hid it under Lexie's bed," she says, and she drops her eyes to the bench beside us.

"The bag with our passports?" I ask her to clarify.

She nods.

"I heard Mommy tell Greg to make sure he packed it in my bag because you couldn't take me to France without it. Lexie didn't want me to leave, and I didn't want to leave, so we snuck into the closet and found them while you were out taking pictures with Sela, and we put them in the blanket box under her bed."

Anger flares.

"And you watched as I and all our other friends frantically searched for them?"

She sniffles. "Yes."

"You realize missing that flight cost me a lot of money."

"I'm sorry. You can have all the money in my piggy bank to pay it back," she mutters.

"Cobie, this is very serious. You're in a lot of trouble. Your mother and I are going to have to discuss your punishment."

"I know, and Santa won't forgive me either, and I'll be put on the naughty list," she whimpers.

I hug her to me, and my eyes meet Sela's watery stare.

"I didn't say I wouldn't forgive you. Just because I punish you doesn't mean I don't forgive you, but being forgiven doesn't always mean you escape the consequences of your actions. Do you understand?" I tell her in a much calmer tone.

She nods as she holds my neck.

"Come on. Let's go back to the inn, and we'll talk about this more in the morning."

I stand with her in my arms, and she keeps her tight grip on me as the three of us walk in silence with only the sound of the soft crunch of the snow beneath our feet.

By the time we reach the front steps of the inn, she is fast asleep.

Sela opens the door for me, and I march straight to our room and lay her on the bed.

She turns on her side and cradles her pillow.

I step back into the hall and shut the door quietly behind me.

Sela is propped against the wall, her face still glistening from her own tears.

I blow out a breath and lean against the wall next to her.

"That was intense," she whispers.

"Yeah, I wasn't quite sure how to handle the situation," I admit.

"For what it's worth, I think you did a pretty good job," she says.

"Thanks."

"You know, you still have time to make it to Paris before Christmas," she says.

For some reason, the thought doesn't appeal to me anymore.

I shake my head. "Why would I force her to go when she went through all this to avoid having to go with me?"

"That's not it," she murmurs.

"Yes, it is. I should have let her stay at home with her mother and baby brother. I was being selfish."

She pushes off the wall and faces me. "Yes, but not in the way you're making it out to be. No, she obviously didn't care to go to Paris. Not because she didn't want to be with you, but because she wouldn't have known another soul. When you're little, you look forward to spending time with family and friends during Christmas. You want to do the cheesy holiday traditions—baking cookies, singing carols, building snowmen, and playing an angel in a live nativity with ornery donkeys."

I laugh.

"One day, she'll be a teenager who wants nothing more than to Instagram her fabulous trip to Paris for her frenemies to drool over, but that time is not now. Trust me, when the time comes, the last thing she's going to want to do is hide something so that she's stranded with her father for four weeks in a row."

"How do you know so much about what kids want?" I ask as she steps into me and wraps her arms around my neck.

"Because I was once an eight-year-old girl who adored her daddy too."

"I just wanted to make this a memorable Christmas since I'd missed all the others."

"Then, congratulations. You succeeded. I'm pretty sure the year you were stranded in Lake Mistletoe is going to be in the top five stories she tells her own children one day."

She's right. This is definitely a year for the books.

"You want to go toast the newlyweds with me?" I ask her.

She smiles. "I thought you'd never ask. There is a glass of Alice's eggnog with my name on it."

Chapter Twenty-Five

Isaac

WE JOIN THE OTHERS OUT IN THE ATRIUM.

I give my apologies for the hubbub and explain what happened to them all.

"Aww, I think it's sweet. She wanted to stay here with us," Willa says.

"I agree," Trixie chimes in.

Keller rolls his eyes. "Between her and Mom, this baby is going to get away with everything," he mutters to me.

Trixie stands. "I want to show you something. I'll be right back."

She walks inside the inn and emerges a few minutes later with a tiny bottle in her hand.

"This is a wishing bottle. The kids wrote their Christmas wishes and placed them inside. Annette and I have been opening them and cataloging the wishes so we can help spread the magic on Christmas Day."

She hands the glass bottle to me. "That's Cobie's wish. You should read it."

I pull the cork from the top of the bottle, turn it upside down, and shake.

The paper doesn't budge.

"It's lodged in there pretty tight. She wrote an entire paragraph and shoved it in," Trixie says.

Sela takes the bottle and uses her nails to clasp the rolled slip of paper and tugs it loose.

I spread it out on the table in front of me and read my daughter's words.

Santa,

I know you're probably upset with me because you didn't need my help finding a way to keep us here, but I wanted to make sure Daddy and I didn't leave before you saw my wish. I don't want to go to France. I've tried to tell him a bunch of times, but he doesn't hear me. I don't like airplanes very much, and I don't want to go someplace where I don't understand what they are saying. I want to stay here in Lake Mistletoe. Daddy laughs and smiles here. He plays with me. He's happy. And that's my Christmas wish. For Daddy to be happy. Thank you for reading this and for keeping my secret even though I know that you know.

Love,
Cobie Ralston

I stare at the words written in her handwriting.

I've tried to tell him a bunch of times, but he doesn't hear me.

Shit.

"It's my fault she went to such extremes," I mutter.

"Don't beat yourself up too badly. There isn't a parent alive who hasn't brushed off their child's words at some point. I did it a thousand times with Hannah," Trudy consoles.

"That is true," Hannah confirms.

"No parent is perfect. We're all just figuring it out as we go along. Next time, you'll do better," Bob offers.

"So, um, what are you gonna do?" Bran asks.

"I'm going to play Santa," I say.

I look to Alice. "Are you okay with giving up your room a bit longer?"

She smiles wide. "Absolutely."

I drive Sela home.

As I walk her inside, my mind tries to come up with the words I want to say to her.

But as we make it to the top of the stairs, I lose all train of thought when she turns and her mouth finds mine immediately. She hungrily kisses me as she pulls me over the threshold and back to the foot of her bed.

All the tension from the evening's events leaves me as her hands slide down and around to cup my behind. I take control of the kiss as she strips her leggings off and wraps her legs around my waist, and I lower her to the mattress. Her head falls back against the pillows, and she arches her back and slides her sweater over her head. She reaches for me, and I move on top of her as she threads her fingers through my hair and tugs. She presses her body into mine, and the evidence of my need twitches against the creamy skin of her thigh as an all-consuming heat crawls up my spine.

Her body starts trembling with desire, and she hooks a leg behind me as she tries desperately to get closer.

I bear up on an elbow for a split second, grab the back of my collar, and fling my shirt over my head and across the room. Then, my attention goes to her breast. She slides her hands down my rib cage and to my hips, the tips of her fingers digging into the muscle.

I release a guttural groan as my tongue runs circles around one taut nipple before I suck it between my teeth and bite down gently. Her body spasms at the contact, and pride bubbles in my chest at the knowledge that I can cause that response in her.

How can I feel this intensely for someone I've only known for a couple of weeks?

Never have my mind and body been so in tune with that of a lover. I want to touch and kiss and possess every inch of her.

She grips me closer as she slides a hand between us and undoes the button of my jeans while my mouth continues to explore her.

An urgent ache pulses in my lower back as she wraps her fingers around my cock.

Damn, that feels so good.

She purrs her encouragement as she struggles to release me from my underwear.

I lift my head at the sound, and before she can protest, I go to my knees and yank my jeans down my thighs, taking my boxers with them.

She sighs as I come back over her.

"Sela." Her name is a lust-filled plea on my lips.

She bears up and takes my mouth as her hand finds me hard and ready once again. She grips the base with one hand as she strokes me firmly with the other. Running her nail over the sensitive tip. I twitch in her fist, and my breath catches as I watch her hands.

"Sela," I rasp once more as my hands clasp her shoulders tightly, and I stare into her eyes.

Her tongue darts out and licks my bottom lip as she continues to stroke me faster.

"Yes," she murmurs, and the heat in her eyes as she watches me nearly sets me aflame.

She grins and falls back against the pillows as I mutter unintelligible sentences.

She begins to rock her hips against my thighs with the rhythm of her hand as she pumps her fist around me.

That's when my patience snaps. I flip her to her back, and she lets out a yelp as her back hits the mattress.

"My turn," I say.

I begin to kiss my way down her body at a maddeningly slow pace. Stroking and caressing every exposed inch until she's a desperate, quivering wreck, writhing beneath my touch.

When I reach her navel, I dip my tongue inside as my hand finds the apex of her thighs.

I growl low and deep when I find her core wet and ready for me. I rake a finger across her, bring it to my lips, and lick it clean.

Her breathing speeds up, and then she moans my name as my mouth devours her.

I spread her apart with my fingers, and my tongue explores her intimate flesh.

She arches up and cries, "Yes. Right there."

Desire ripples down my spine as I lift my eyes to watch as she loses control.

My name tears from her lips as I nip at her clit with my teeth, and her hips involuntarily jump in my hold. Her muscles clench as I insert a finger and start to curl it in and out, searching for that perfect spot. I take my time using my mouth, tongue, and hands to drive her into a frenzy. She sinks her fingers into my scalp and holds me where she wants me as she thrusts her hips to meet my tongue until her legs are shaking uncontrollably. I bring my eyes to hers and hold her gaze as she falls over the edge, gasping my name over and over as her orgasm rockets through her.

As she lies there, catching her breath and recovering, I push up off of the end of the bed, retrieve a foil packet from my discarded jeans, and return to her, placing one knee on the bed as I tear the packet open with my teeth and slowly sheathe myself.

She sits up and takes my hand, pulling me on top of her. Her hot, slick, bared skin against mine. I guide my erection to her entrance, and with one swift thrust of my hips, I enter her. Filling her completely.

And she lets out a satisfied sigh.

I reach back and clasp one of her ankles and tug it over my shoulder so I can move deeper and faster inside her.

She flings her head back into the pillows.

I lean my head so I can kiss her exposed neck, and the sensation of the gentle kiss in contrast to the pounding rhythm is just what it takes to bring her back to the brink of release.

Her breath starts coming in short, hard pants as her legs begin to tremble, and she locks them securely behind me.

"Sela," I grunt as her muscles begin to tighten around me.

I grip her hips as I begin thrusting rapidly. She slides a hand down my side, grazing me with her fingernails before digging them into the curve of my ass and holding on as I come close to the edge.

I know she is close, too, so I slip one hand between us, pinching her in just the right spot.

That does it.

Her body begins to convulse as I hoarsely shout her name.

I think I love her.

The words are on the tip of my tongue as I watch her fall apart.

I quickly lose my hold on control, and my tightly coiled climax explodes into her.

I bring my mouth to hers as my pleasure takes over.

We lie here, tangled for several moments, drained of all strength. Her trapped beneath me, taking my weight as she strokes my back lightly.

Chapter Twenty-Six

Isaac

I ASK SELA TO COME TO THE INN FOR BREAKFAST BEFORE I KISS HER one last time and get dressed.

I don't want to leave her, but I need to be there when Cobie wakes up. She has to know that I love her, no matter what, and that even when she does something bad, that fact will never change.

I take my time driving back as I contemplate what to say to my little one. I wish her mother were here. Lonnie is so much better at these moments than I am, but it's time I learn how to talk, and listen to, my daughter.

All is quiet when I enter the inn so I tiptoe down the hallway and slowly open the door to our room, trying not to make a sound. Gathering a pair of clean sweatpants and a tee, I make my way into the adjoining bathroom and shower and dress quickly. Then, I crawl in beside my little girl, tuck her close, and join her in sleep.

When I feel movement at my side, I open an eye to find Cobie staring at me. Her head propped on her tiny fists.

"Are you awake, Daddy?" she whispers.

"I am now," I croak.

"I have a surprise for you," she says.

"What's that?"

She clasps my arm and tugs as hard as she can.

"Get up and see," she commands.

I sit up and wipe the sleep from my eyes as I take her in fully.

She's dressed with her coat and mittens on. Both of our suitcases are standing by the door, and the navy bag is protruding from the front pocket of mine.

I raise an eyebrow at her.

"I got up and got us all ready to go to Paris," she says. "See?" She tilts her head toward the luggage.

I cross my arms over my chest and watch her.

"Come on, Daddy. It's almost eleven, and we have to go now if we want to catch our plane."

I have to bite the inside of my cheek to keep from chuckling.

"Cobie, come here," I say in a stern voice once I have control of myself.

Her lip quivers. "But we have to go to the airport," she murmurs as she twists her hands nervously.

"We're not going to the airport today. We don't have any flights booked for today."

"But you can call them in the car and tell them we're on our way," she says.

I nod. "You're right. I could do that, but I'm not going to."

Her eyes fall to the floor. "Are you going to take me home to Mommy?" she asks.

"No, I'm not. Come here," I demand.

She shuffles her feet until she is standing beside me. Her eyes still trained on the floor.

"Why would I take you home before Christmas?" I ask.

She sniffles. "Because I hid our passports and lied to you," she mumbles.

"Didn't you tell me you were sorry for doing that last night?"

She nods.

"I owe you an apology too," I tell her.

She looks up at me with wide, red-rimmed eyes. "You do?"

"Yes, baby, I do. I was so excited to take you on a trip that I didn't listen when you tried to tell me you didn't want to go. I'm sorry. I'll do better at the listening thing. But you have to promise not to take things that don't belong to you and not to lie anymore."

"I pinkie swear promise," she yells as she throws her arms around me.

I squeeze her tightly, and when I release her, she looks up at me.

"Now that we've gotten everything out in the open, the question is, what are we going to do for Christmas?"

She swipes at her nose and waits for me to answer my own question.

"Since we're already here and our friends have been so kind to us, I think we should probably stay in Lake Mistletoe. What do you think?"

Her eyes light up. "I think that's a great idea, Daddy," she squeals.

"There is one condition though," I add.

She climbs on the bed and sits beside me.

"You have to give everyone an apology for lying, especially Lexie because you talked her into hiding your bad deeds, and that wasn't very fair, was it?"

"No, sir. It wasn't fair at all. I'll apologize to everyone at breakfast," she says.

I smile at her and pull her into my arms.

"I love you to the moon and back, baby," I say.

"I love you to the stars and back," she says.

We unpack our bags, and I get dressed before we join everyone in the dining room.

Trixie, Alice, Annette, Willa, Keller, Lexie and her parents, and a few other guests of the inn, as well as Dawn, Daniel, Norah, and Sela are all seated around the table, enjoying bacon and pancakes when we walk in.

"Good morning, everybody. Cobie has something she'd like to say to you all before we sit to eat," I say, drawing their attention.

She clings to my leg as she starts to talk. "I'm sorry I stole my daddy's bag and hid it and that everybody had to spend so much time looking for it. And I'm really sorry I got you into trouble, Lexie."

She turns to face Lexie's parents. "Please don't be mad at her. She was just being a good friend."

Then, she turns to Trixie and Willa. "I hope you can forgive me and that we can stay here for Christmas."

Sela's eyes dart to mine. And I smile.

Trixie climbs out of her chair and reaches a hand to Cobie. Cobie takes it, and the woman tugs her into a hug.

"Of course we forgive you, and we'd love for you to stay and have Christmas with us."

Trixie turns her to the table. "Isn't that right?" she asks, and everyone chimes in with positive feedback.

"Now that that's settled, let's get you some pancakes," Alice says as she takes a fork and piles three golden cakes onto a plate for Cobie.

I slide into the open chair at Sela's side, and my hand finds hers under the table.

"Do you happen to need a date for the Holly Ball?" I ask.

"Why? Do you have somebody in mind?"

I turn and plant a kiss on her lips in full view of everyone.

"Now, that's what I'm talking about. Christmas magic," Norah shouts.

Epilogue

Sela
Four Months Later

"**H**URRY UP, SELA. YOU DON'T WANT TO BE LATE," NORAH calls up the stairs.

I double-check my purse one last time to make sure my passport is tucked inside.

Clicking off the lights and locking the door, I drag my suitcase to the flower shop.

"I'm ready," I say.

Mom gives me a quick hug. "Have fun and take lots of pictures. And don't forget to text your father to let us know you landed safely."

"I will, I promise."

My phone rings, and I look down to see it's Isaac calling.

"Hey," I say as I accept the call.

"Are you on the road yet?" he asks.

"I'm just saying my good-byes now," I tell him.

He chuckles. "They do realize you're only going to be gone for two weeks, right?"

He's already in Paris on assignment. I'm flying to San Antonio to pick up Cobie, and she and I are joining him there for spring break.

Paris in the spring has always been a dream of mine.

"I keep telling them that."

"Tell them all that I said hello and that we'll be back home before Easter. And then get in the car so Bran can get you to the airport."

Home.

Isaac Ralston calls Lake Mistletoe home now, and when he's not traveling for *Epic Odysseys* or to San Antonio to visit Cobie, he is here with me.

I can still remember the moment he told me at last year's Holly Ball.

"So, what happens now?" I asked.

"You ground me, and I show you the world."

Preview of

Stone

HEARTS

Prologue

DALLAS
Six Years Ago

SWEET JESUS, THIS LITTLE MONSTER IS RIPPING HIS WAY OUT OF ME. I've never felt pain like this before. When he finally makes it, he's getting his first time-out for trying to take all his momma's insides with him as he exits my body.

"Breathe, Dallas," Momma coaxes.

I tightly squeeze her hand as another contraction hits me like a freight train. The pain shoots down my spine and explodes in my pelvis.

"I *am* breathing, Momma," I scream.

"No, you're not, sweetheart," she says gently.

I cut my eyes to her and bite through gritted teeth. "Yes. I. Am."

"Whoa, I think her head spun around on that one. Did you hear that demon inside her?"

I whip my head around to my stupid brother, Payne, who has his iPhone pointed directly at me.

Why in the hell did I agree to have him in the room while I expelled a human torture device from my vagina?

"You shut the hell up and remember to stay north of the Mason–Dixon Line with that thing, asshole," I spew in his direction.

He just grins at me.

"Payne, dear, I think we might have to switch."

Momma is gently trying to tug her hand from my death grip. Her expression is one of intense pain, and the tips of her fingers are starting to turn purple. I let go as the contraction eases, and she hurries back from my bedside.

"Sure thing, Momma. I can handle it," Payne says as he hands the phone off to our mother. He plops down in the seat beside me and raises his right arm to me in an arm-wrestling challenge.

The doctor looks up from between my legs and pipes in, "He's crowning."

"Well, it's about time. I thought he had decided to stay in there until college," I spit out just as another contraction starts to ripple through me.

I grab hold of Payne's hand and nearly stand up in the bed. He starts trying to play thumb war with me, and I reach over and grab his thumb with my other hand and bend it back as hard as I can.

"Shit!" he yells. "I think you broke my thumb. That hurt like hell."

"Oh, really? Is a head the size of a bowling ball trying to break its way out of your pee hole? No? Then, suck it up, pansy-ass!"

"Children. Let's be nice. We don't want the baby watching his birth video and hearing you two cursing and fighting," Momma interjects.

"Give me one more big push, Dallas," the doctor commands before I can release my wrath on my mother.

Payne stands and grabs my hand harder. "Come on, sis. You've got this. Little man is almost here. One, two, three …" he counts as I bear down as hard as I can and push with all the strength I have left.

"He's out," the nurse excitedly announces just as I hear the first soft cry ring through the room.

"Oh my goodness, he's perfect!" Momma cries as I try to muster the energy to raise my head and look at him.

Before I have a chance, the doctor asks if anyone wants to cut the cord. I look up at Payne, and he is pale as a ghost.

Momma lays her hand on my shoulder and steps around to the doctor. "I do," she says tearfully.

A few seconds later, a gooey, bald bright red mess of screaming baby is laid on my chest.

His eyes are closed, and he is unhappy.

"Hey now, mister," I coo at him as I bring my hand to his face. "What's all that racket about? I'm the one who had her hoo-ha ripped in half, not you."

His eyes pop open as he starts to settle, and his little head moves to bring his face closer to my voice.

"There you are," I whisper. "You must be the one who's been playing soccer with my bladder the last three months, huh? You've already bought yourself extra chores until you're twenty-one, buddy."

He grunts at me and blinks his eyes shut.

"Already ignoring me, I see."

One eye opens back up, and what looks like a faint smile but is more than likely gas passes over him.

"Playing opossum. Mommy is onto you, Beau Stovall." I cradle him in my arms and plant a kiss on his forehead before nestling him under my chin. "It's you and me, kiddo. We're in this together from here on out. I will love you and protect you with my last breath. Oh, baby boy, we're going to have great adventures, you and me."

I hear a sniffle and look to Momma, who is staring affectionately at the two of us.

I hope that I'm able to be half the mother to him as she has been to me.

One

DALLAS
Present

"OKAY, THERE WE GO." I STEP BACK TO TAKE A LOOK AT MY work.

Beau stands in front of me in his homemade Fly Guy costume for Book Character Day at school. The getup consists of white-and-black bug eyes made of small Styrofoam plates, construction paper adhered to a headband, and cardboard wings attached to a set of Daddy's old suspenders, paired with a brown turtleneck and cords.

He patiently waits, grinning, as I make my assessment, and he is undeniably the cutest little snaggle-toothed bug I have ever seen.

"Perfect!" I squeal as he beams at me.

I gather his lunch box and shoes as he runs to his room to grab his backpack.

"How am I going to get my coat on and get in the truck with my wings?" he asks as he runs back into the living room.

"You'll have to remove the suspenders and ask Mrs. Perry to help you put them back on when you get to your classroom."

He snaps them off and carefully tucks them under his arm. Once we are in the truck, I start our daily routine.

"What day is today, Beau?"

"The best day ever!" he replies.

"Why is it the best day ever?"

"Because we woke up this morning," he answers.

"What are we gonna do today?" I ask.

"We are going to be kind and give everyone our brightest smile."

"What aren't we gonna do?"

"Let anyone steal our shine."

"How much do I love you?"

"All the way up to the moon and back."

"That's right, baby," I confirm and put my right hand in the air for a high five, which he immediately returns.

God, I love this kid.

When I turn the key, the engine makes a horrible grinding noise, and then it rumbles before it stops.

Oh no, please don't do this right now.

I try again. The lights on the dashboard start flashing dimly, and the engine makes a clicking sound but doesn't turn over at all.

I groan, close my eyes, and lightly bang my head against the steering wheel.

A few minutes later, two little arms come around my neck from behind and squeeze.

"It's gonna be okay, Mommy."

I take a deep breath and turn my head to look at his earnest face. His round glasses have slipped down on his nose, and his big brown eyes are fixed on me. I remind myself that this tiny human takes his emotional cues from me, and I don't have the luxury of breaking down. So, I smile at him.

"You're right; it's going to be okay. In fact, I think this old truck just gave me extra time with my favorite boy in the whole wide world this morning."

He beams at me and sits back down as I fish my cell out of the bag. Momma already left for the bakery today, and Payne and Daddy left at the crack of dawn to meet the crop-dusting plane. I could call Sophie, but it would take her a while to get here, and I don't want Beau to be that late on Book Character Day. He'd be devastated if he missed the group class photo. So, I press Myer's name saved in my favorites in my phone and pray he isn't out on the ranch where he can't answer.

"Hey, Dal." His deep, rich voice comes over the line, and I release a relieved breath.

"Hey, Myer. I hate to call this early. I know you're probably busy with the calves, but my truck has crapped out on me again, and I need help getting Beau to school. Momma's at the bakery, and Daddy and Payne are having the fields dusted today."

"Pop can handle things for an hour or so. I'll swing by and pick you guys up in ten."

Myer Wilson is my brother, Payne's best friend. His family owns Stoney Ridge Ranch, which backs up to my family's farm and orchard.

"Thanks, Myer," I say as I collapse in relief.

"No problem. See you soon."

He disconnects, and I turn to Beau.

"Looks like you and I get to have a slice of Nana's apple cake before school."

"Yay! It really is the best day ever, Mommy," he exclaims before he opens his door, hops out, and runs to the porch of our home.

It's a modest home. My daddy and Uncle Jimbo turned one of the old grain silos behind my parents' farmhouse into a one-bedroom loft home for my son and me when my ex-husband was sent to prison on felony drug charges while I was pregnant with Beau. He has the bedroom, and I sleep in the loft that overlooks the open living room and kitchen. It's not big, but it's not tiny either. It fits us just right, and we love it.

I follow Beau inside, help him pop his wings back on so I can snap a few pictures and then I slice us each a piece of cake and pour us a glass of milk. He regales me with made-up stories of Fly Guy's coming adventures of the day while we wait for Myer to arrive.

The knock comes just as we finish up.

"It's open," I call as I rinse our plates.

Myer swings it open, and his blue eyes sweep the room. When they land on Beau, he fakes a start. "Whoa, you scared me there for a minute. Are you a monster?"

"No, silly. I'm Fly Guy. I'm not scary at all. I'm a good friend," Beau informs him.

"Well, it's nice to meet you, Fly Guy. I heard you need a ride to school, but that can't be right. You have wings so you can fly yourself there."

Beau giggles. "They aren't real. See?" He turns around to show Myer the wings stapled to the suspenders. Then, he turns back around and lifts the big eyes off of his head. "It's me, Myer, Beau Stovall. I'm just pretending to be Fly Guy."

"Well, look at that. It is Beau Stovall. That's a good costume. You sure had me fooled."

"I tricked him, Mommy. I bet I'll win the first-place prize!" Beau says excitedly.

"In that case, we'd better get you to school right away," I say in answer.

He nods his head and races past Myer and out the open door.

"Thank you for rescuing me. Again," I offer as I grab my keys and purse from the kitchen island and follow.

"Not a big deal, Dal," he replies warmly as I ease past him.

He shuts the door and takes my keys from my hand to lock the dead bolt behind us as I wrangle my buzzing fly into the backseat of his white Silverado.

A few beats later, he climbs behind the steering wheel in the extended cab and passes me my keys.

"Go ahead and take your truck key off that ring. I'll drop you off at Rustic Peak, and I'll come back and have a look under the hood after lunch today."

Rustic Peak Ranch belongs to my best friend, Sophie's family, and I work there part-time, helping her keep the ranch's books.

"You don't mind?" I ask as I gladly hand over the key.

"Nope. Hopefully, it's something Payne and I can fix ourselves this time. If not, I'll hitch it to my truck, and we'll haul it over to Jackie's garage this evening."

Ugh, just what I need. Another repair bill.

"Don't start worrying now. It could be nothing," he says, reading the look of concern on my face.

"Yeah, Mommy. Don't let that truck steal your shine," Beau chimes in from the backseat.

"I don't think it's possible to steal your momma's shine, little man," Myer replies while looking at Beau in the rearview mirror.

A warm feeling pours over me, and I decide they're right. Me worrying about what's wrong with that old horse of a truck isn't going to change a single thing, so I might as well have myself a fabulous Monday. I'll figure out how to pay for the repairs once I know what they are.

I take my sunglasses from my purse and slide them on, and then I roll the window down and let the cool spring air waft through my hair as I plant a big old smile on my face.

Acknowledgments

Where did the year go?

No, seriously, how can it be November already? I swear as each year slips by the sands fall faster and faster through the narrow passage of the hourglass.

2023 was a year of transition, setbacks, and healing.

I've cried a river of tears and built a mountain of strength.

All of those emotions leaked out onto the pages as I typed the end of book nineteen.

Nineteen.

Wow.

I have a lot of people to thank for helping me get here. My team is a dream team of amazing women. Each one is a valuable cog in the wheels that keep this train running.

I want to thank my editor, Jovana Shirley, for sticking with me this year. I don't make things easy for you Jo, but you never make me feel like the disaster I am and you always make me look good. Your professionalism is only matched by your kindness and grace. I'm so grateful for you and our friendship. Commas are still the devil.

Sommer Stein, here we are again, this cover is a masterpiece. We are so in sync. You always capture the heart of the story with your creations.

Stacey Blake, your interior designs are artful and always capture the spirit of the stories held within the pages.

Autumn Sexton, I always say I could not and would not want to be on this author path without you. You keep me on task, you keep me the train on the tracks, you step in when I need you and you make everything possible. You are an incredible publicist. A priceless friend and love you more. Thank you for all you do.

I owe a debt of gratitude to My "&" Girls, The Hens, my family and friends, and especially all of you, the readers. Thank you for your support and encouragement. Sharing stories of hope and healing with you all is what I live for. I hope they have helped heal you all in some way just as they have me. Thank you for continuing to show up.

Last but not least, I want to thank my husband, David, for allowing me the freedom to chase my dreams while being my safe place. I love you more with each passing year.

Cheers to a new year and all the stories I hope to bring to you guys. Happy Holidays!

other books

Cross My Heart Duet

Both of Me

Both of Us

Poplar Falls

Rustic Hearts

Stone Hearts

Wicked Hearts

Fragile Hearts

Merry Hearts

Crazy Hearts

Knitted Hearts

Lake Mistletoe Series

Lake Mistletoe

Smitten in Lake Mistletoe

Stranded in Lake Mistletoe

The Balsam Ridge Series

Life After Wife

Fate After Fame

Rain After Fire

Hope After Loss

Rise After Fall

Cozy After Snow

about
the author

Amber Kelly is a romance author that calls North Carolina home. She has been a avid reader from a young age and you could always find her with her nose in a book completely enthralled in an adventure. With the support of her husband and family, in 2018, she decided to finally give a voice to the stories in her head and her debut novel, Both of Me was born. You can connect with Amber on Facebook at facebook. com/AuthorAmberKelly, on IG @authoramberkelly, on twitter @ AuthorAmberKel1 or via her website www.authoramberkelly.com.

Made in the USA
Monee, IL
23 December 2024

75203576R00129